W9-BRW-730

"Are you okay?" he asked.

She relaxed her grimace. "I'm fine." She leaned forward and began to tie the laces of the boot. "I just want to get out of here." Their eyes met and she held his gaze. "Then you and I need to talk."

They had a lot of things they could talk about, but Dillon had no idea what he would say to her. His earlier anger had been overshadowed by his concern for her and the physical memory of how good they had been together. She finished lacing the boot and he bent to take her arm. "Lean on me all you want to," he said.

She nodded, and he pulled her to her feet and she leaned against him, pressed to his side. She felt different. Rounder. He glanced down and what he saw shook him, though he remained steady, still supporting her. She put a protective hand on her rounded belly. "That's what we need to talk about," she said. "I'm pregnant, and the baby is definitely yours."

ALPHA TRACKER

CINDI MYERS

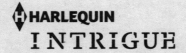

If you purchased this book without a cover you should be aware that this book is stolen property. It was reported as "unsold and destroyed" to the publisher, and neither the author nor the publisher has received any payment for this "stripped book."

For Carol and Podrick

Special thanks and acknowledgment are given to Cindi Myers for her contribution to the K-9s on Patrol miniseries.

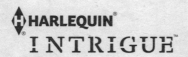

Recycling programs for this product may not exist in your area.

ISBN-13: 978-1-335-58199-0

Alpha Tracker

Copyright © 2022 by Harlequin Enterprises ULC

All rights reserved. No part of this book may be used or reproduced in any manner whatsoever without written permission except in the case of brief quotations embodied in critical articles and reviews.

This is a work of fiction. Names, characters, places and incidents are either the product of the author's imagination or are used fictitiously. Any resemblance to actual persons, living or dead, businesses, companies, events or locales is entirely coincidental.

For questions and comments about the quality of this book, please contact us at CustomerService@Harlequin.com.

Harlequin Enterprises ULC
22 Adelaide St. West, 41st Floor
Toronto, Ontario M5H 4E3, Canada
www.Harlequin.com

Printed in U.S.A.

Cindi Myers is the author of more than fifty novels. When she's not plotting new romance story lines, she enjoys skiing, gardening, cooking, crafting and daydreaming. A lover of small-town life, she lives with her husband and two spoiled dogs in the Colorado mountains.

Books by Cindi Myers

Harlequin Intrigue

Alpha Tracker

Eagle Mountain: Search for Suspects

Disappearance at Dakota Ridge
Conspiracy in the Rockies
Missing at Full Moon Mine
Grizzly Creek Standoff

The Ranger Brigade: Rocky Mountain Manhunt

Investigation in Black Canyon
Mountain of Evidence
Mountain Investigation
Presumed Deadly

Eagle Mountain Murder Mystery: Winter Storm Wedding

Ice Cold Killer
Snowbound Suspicion
Cold Conspiracy
Snowblind Justice

Eagle Mountain Murder Mystery

Saved by the Sheriff
Avalanche of Trouble
Deputy Defender
Danger on Dakota Ridge

Visit the Author Profile page at Harlequin.com.

CAST OF CHARACTERS

Roslyn Kern—The former DJ is putting her life back together after a year of heartache, determined to make things right with the man who helped her heal.

Dillon Diaz—The police sergeant and search and rescue volunteer hasn't been able to forget the mystery woman he spent one incredible weekend with.

Bentley—Trained in search and rescue, this Australian shepherd is gentle and loyal, but determined to protect those he loves.

Kent Anderson—The escaped mass killer has vowed to take out anyone who gets in his way as he flees through the wilderness.

Colleen Diaz—Dillon's mother has a knack for getting her way and will fight for her family's happiness.

Chapter One

If Roslyn Kern had been the superstitious type, she might have taken the ominous clouds of smoke gathering in the distance beyond Jasper, Idaho, as a bad omen. But she wasn't superstitious, she reminded herself, only nervous and uncertain what the outcome of this visit to Jasper might be. She didn't want to be here, but part of being an adult meant doing things that scared you. She had been doing a lot of that lately.

"Next!" The young woman behind the counter at Millard's Diner summoned her forward. The diner at the corner of Main and Second was busy with both table and counter service on this Friday before the Fourth of July, but everyone around Roslyn seemed in a good mood. "What can I get you?" the clerk asked.

Roslyn looked longingly at the latte the previous customer was carrying away, then ordered an herbal tea. "Would you like a blueberry muffin to go with that?" the woman asked. "They're fresh out of the oven."

Roslyn's stomach rumbled. "Yes, please," she said.

The clerk rang up her sale and accepted Roslyn's debit card. "Are you here for the holiday weekend?" the clerk asked as they waited for the card machine to process the charge.

"Yes," Roslyn said. "Do you think the fire is going to head this way?" The smell of smoke lingered in the air, though maybe Roslyn was more sensitive to the odor than most.

"I know it looks close, but the fire is a long way away," the woman said. She returned Roslyn's card. "There's a ridge between us and the blaze, though if the wind shifts..." She shrugged. "The firefighters are keeping an eye on things. I'm not too worried."

Roslyn nodded and moved on to accept her muffin and tea from another server. She spotted a small table against the side wall and headed for it. She had arrived in town late last night from Chicago and hadn't had much time to formulate a plan. She needed to find Dillon, but wasn't certain where to begin. Should she start with the police? She shook her head. No, not unless there was no other way. The first time she saw him, she wanted a situation that was more private.

She tore a piece from the muffin and popped it into her mouth, savoring the sweet cake surrounding a single juicy berry. She would have to stop in again tomorrow for another muffin. It almost made the tea bearable. She gazed out the window at the town of Jasper. She had visited the Chamber of Commerce website before she planned her trip, but the photos

there of broad streets framed by Western-style build-
ings with wooden false fronts and Victorian brick-
work hadn't captured the flavor of the bustling town.
The sidewalks were filled with people, most of whom
appeared to be vacationers enjoying the sunny July
day in spite of the distant smoke clouds. Barrels of
pink and white and purple petunias dotted the sidewalks, and hanging baskets of red verbena and blue
lobelia hung from every light post. Red, white and
blue bunting draped storefronts and a banner over
the street welcomed everyone to the annual Indepen-
dence Day celebration.

A flyer in the bed-and-breakfast where she was
staying had advertised a dance, a parade, a rodeo
and fireworks as part of the weekend's festivities.
Roslyn wondered if she would be in any mood to
celebrate once she had accomplished what she had
come here to do.

She realized she was searching the crowd for Dillon's handsome face. Her heart beat a little faster
at the idea that he might be close by. She had such
a clear picture of him in her mind—tall, broad-
shouldered, with olive skin, sculpted cheekbones
and close-cropped brown hair. He had captivated
her from the moment they rode a lift chair together
at the nearby Brundage Mountain Resort. He had
been so easy to talk to and they had ended up skiing
the rest of the day together, having dinner together,
then going back to her hotel room.

They had spent the whole weekend in a magical
bubble. She had come to the ski resort in McCall

feeling broken and fragile, only a few weeks past a humiliating public breakup with her fiancé and the loss of a job she had loved. Thanks to a wonderful two days and nights with Dillon, she'd left feeling stronger than she had in weeks. He had been just what she needed during an awful time in her life. Saying goodbye to him had been hard, but the short time she'd spent with him had given her the strength she needed to go back to Chicago and clean up the mess she had left behind. She would always be grateful to him for that.

She had delayed coming here to find him because she wanted to keep that beautiful memory unspoiled, but life had a way of interfering with the best of plans. She needed to talk to him, and she couldn't put it off much longer. Jasper was a small town, so she had thought finding him wouldn't be that difficult. But now that she was here, she wasn't so sure. Maybe if she sat here long enough, he would walk through the café door, and give her that smile that warmed her clear to her toes, his hazel green eyes sparking with delight. She turned toward the doorway, almost expecting to see him there. Instead, she was startled to see another familiar face.

"Roslyn? Oh my gosh—what are you doing here?" Cheri Benton, one of Roslyn's best friends, rushed forward to greet her, followed by her boyfriend, Buck, and another couple.

"Amber and Wes, this is Roslyn," Cheri made the introductions.

Roslyn stood and shook hands with everyone.

"We're staying in McCall for the weekend and came over here to hike," Cheri explained. "Kind of a last-minute trip to get out of the city, you know?"

"You made such a big deal about how much you enjoyed your visit to the area this winter that we wanted to check it out," added Buck.

"It's a last-minute trip for me, too." Roslyn latched on to this convenient explanation for her presence here. "I had some time free, so I figured, why not?"

"Yeah, you'd better relax while you can, right?"

"Where are you planning to hike?" Roslyn asked, anxious to steer the conversation away from herself. Not that Cheri and Buck weren't good friends, but they didn't know everything about her life, and she didn't want them to know the real reason she was in Jasper. Not yet.

"There's a trailhead not far from here that leads up into the mountains," Buck said. "The Williams Gap Trail. There's supposed to be a lot of wildflowers this time of year."

"You should come with us," Cheri said. "You're up for it, right?"

"Of course," Roslyn said. She had hiking boots and a water bottle in her car. "If you're not going too far."

"Not far at all," Cheri said. "You should definitely come."

"Come on," Buck agreed. "It will give us a chance to catch up."

It had only been a couple of weeks since Roslyn had been to Cheri and Buck's apartment for dinner, but she appreciated his warm invitation. "I would like to come with you," she said.

"Great," Cheri said. "We'll grab some coffees to go and head out. You can ride with us."

While they waited for coffee, Roslyn gathered her belongings. The hike wouldn't take long—not more than a couple of hours. Maybe in that time she could come up with a plan for finding and approaching Dillon. What she had to say to him would be a shock. He probably wouldn't like it. She needed the extra time to prepare herself for what would probably be another rejection. It wouldn't be the first time a man had turned his back on her. She straightened her spine and smoothed her loose tunic. She shouldn't anticipate trouble. Whatever happened with Dillon, she would deal with it. She'd been getting very good at looking after herself lately—the one good thing that had come out of the disaster she had made of her life so far.

SERGEANT DILLON DIAZ guided his pickup into one of the last open parking slots in front of Daniels Canine Academy. Even from here he could see half a dozen people moving among the kennels and around the main building that housed the dog training facility. Why all the activity on a Friday morning of a holiday weekend?

He opened the truck door. "Come on, Bentley," he called.

Bentley, a four-year-old black-and-white Australian shepherd, leaped to the ground and danced a circle around Dillon, tongue hanging out in an excited doggy grin. "You know where you are, don't you, boy?" Dillon asked, and bent to pat the dog's side. Bentley had spent many hours training at the academy for his work as a search and rescue canine. "We're just stopping in to say hello today."

Bentley trotted beside Dillon up the gravel path toward the DCA office, ears pricked to take in the excited barking of dogs and the murmur of human voices that filled the air. Dillon pushed open the door to the office and administrator Barbara Macy looked up. A pleasant, middle-aged woman with long brown hair, Barbara kept everything at DCA running smoothly. Her frown transformed into a smile as she recognized him. "Hey, Dillon," she called. "And hello, Bentley."

Bentley wagged his plumed tail and trotted toward the desk. "What's all the commotion?" Dillon asked, closing the door behind him.

"We're prepping kennels to take in dogs from people who might have to evacuate for the fire," Barbara said. "We got word this morning that there are some neighborhoods on the periphery of the national forest that authorities would like to clear out just in case the wind shifts suddenly. What can I do for you?"

"I was hoping to speak with Emma," he said. "But it's not urgent. I can come back another time."

Barbara stood. "Let me get her. I know she'll want to see you." She disappeared through a door at the back of the office.

The door to the outside opened and Piper Lambert, Emma's chief assistant in training the dogs, bustled in. She wore her long red hair in a braid trailing down her back, and a harried expression on her face. "Has anyone seen the extra folding kennels? They're supposed to be in the barn but we can't find them." She looked around the room, frowning, until her gaze came to rest on Dillon. "Hello, Dillon. What are you doing here? And where is everybody else?"

"Barbara went to fetch Emma. I stopped by with a question for her, but I didn't expect you to be so busy."

"It's a bit chaotic this morning, but nothing new about that," Piper said. "Any news about the fire? I've been too busy to keep up."

Dillon pulled out his phone and checked the latest fire report. The InciWeb site, which tracked wildfires on public lands, listed the blaze as the Gem Creek fire. "InciWeb says the fire grew overnight to just under ten thousand acres, but it's still well west of Jasper, confined to national forest land."

"That's still too close for comfort to some of those neighborhoods to the north," Piper said. "I expect we'll be getting a lot of evacuees."

"Probably." People around here had learned to be cautious and prepare for the worst, even while putting faith in wildland firefighting crews to keep the flames away from houses and towns.

The door at the back of the room opened and Barbara returned, followed by Emma Daniels, whose light brown hair was pulled back in a ponytail. The founder of Daniels Canine Academy, Emma had established a reputation as one of the finest dog trainers in the West, as well as a generous and giving member of the community. "Hello, Bentley." In typical fashion, Emma greeted the dog first, then looked up to smile at Dillon. "Hello, stranger. What brings you here?"

Piper had already turned to ask Barbara about the missing kennels. The two of them left to check the storage shed where Barbara thought they had been moved, leaving Emma and Dillon alone. "I didn't mean to interrupt when you're so busy," Dillon said.

"When are we not busy?" Emma asked. "What can I do for you?"

"I wanted to see if you knew anything about wilderness tracking training for Bentley," Dillon said. "He's been great for search and rescue work, but I was thinking the wilderness training would be useful in some of the places we have to search."

Emma nodded. "Those courses focus on the kind of rough country we have here." She walked over to a filing cabinet and opened a drawer. "I'm sure I have some information here somewhere."

"Don't bother with it now," Dillon said. "I can get the information later. Barbara told me you're going to be taking in evacuees."

"We're part of the county's emergency management plan," she said. "The fairgrounds over in McCall take horses and other livestock. We try to take as many dogs as possible, to free up the animal shelter in town for cats and birds and other small animals. There isn't enough room in the evacuation centers for people and their pets, so people need to know there's a safe place for their animals. Otherwise, some of them would simply refuse to evacuate."

"What happens if the fire heads this way?" Dillon asked.

"We have a plan for that, too." She gestured behind her. "We've got a whole row of trailers back there we can use to transport kennels with dogs, and even more volunteers to help load and drive. But we're hoping it doesn't come to that. I hear the state is sending in a slurry bomber and another team of hotshots to battle the blaze."

The door to the office opened and William, one of the at-risk teens Emma had hired to work for her, stepped in. Dillon had lost count of the young people Emma had helped over the years. She had a knack for seeing past the full-sleeve tattoos, ear gauges and bad attitudes to the individuals who needed a safe place in the world. "Emma, do you want Atlas and Ridger together, or Atlas and Tassie?" William asked.

"Put Tassie in with Atlas—he'll do better with a female," Emma said. "Put Ridger in with Petra. Those two get along. Did you and Hugh get those portable kennels out of storage?"

"Yes, ma'am. Hugh and Kyle are setting them up now."

"Great. Thank you."

William nodded and ducked out of the office once more.

Emma turned back to Dillon. "Are you on duty this afternoon?"

He shook his head. "I'm off today. I'm working the rest of the weekend, though."

"Then I'll probably see you again. My understanding is the police department has agreed to help with evacuations. Be sure and reassure people that they can trust me with their dogs."

"I'll let them know their pets couldn't be in better hands."

"Check back next week and I'll have some information for you about the wilderness training." She looked down at Bentley, who had been sitting at her feet, blue eyes fixed on her. Emma smiled and pulled a treat from her pocket. "Good boy," she said and handed it to him.

Man and dog left the office. Dillon wondered if he should call the police department and ask if the chief wanted him to report for a shift. He shook his head. If he was needed, someone would call. And with the town full of tourists and the smoke from the fire having everyone on edge, he would be plenty busy the rest of the holiday weekend. He should enjoy his time off while he could. Maybe he'd take Bentley for a hike.

Or he could spend part of the day online, searching for the elusive Rosie Kenley. As many times as he told himself he needed to forget about the woman he had spent all of two nights—and two amazing days—with five months ago, he couldn't shake this desire—this need—to find her. Rosie and he had had a wonderful time together—an amazing time. He had been sure when they parted that they would see each other again, but she had simply vanished. Months of searching hadn't turned up anything so far, but nobody was anonymous these days. He just had to find the right place to look.

And what was he going to do when he found her? Her failure to try to get in touch with him for five months was a pretty clear indication she wasn't interested in seeing him again. The thought stung. He had been sure she had felt the same strong connection between them that had stunned him, but then she had simply disappeared.

There was also the big chance that Rosie had something to hide. As a cop, he had had plenty of experience trying to track down missing persons, but so far she had eluded him. She had said she was single—recently split from someone. But maybe she and her former boyfriend had gotten back together. Maybe she was even married now, with a new name. That would explain some of his difficulty locating her.

He started the truck and looked over his shoulder at Bentley, whose harness was fastened securely in the back seat. "I don't like unanswered questions," he said. The dog pricked his ears, focused intently on Dillon.

Dillon faced forward again, checked the backing camera and pulled out of the parking spot. A need to solve puzzles made him a good cop, but it also made it impossible for him to let things go. He had unfinished business with Rosie Kenley, and he wouldn't rest easy until it was settled.

Chapter Two

"This is so gorgeous!" Cheri swept her arm wide to indicate the field of wildflowers spread out before them. Magenta paintbrushes, purple lupines, scarlet gilia, golden sunflowers and more painted a tapestry against a backdrop of dark green conifers and granite peaks. Even the clouds of smoke rising in the distance didn't detract from the beauty of the scene.

"It's amazing." Roslyn studied the flowers through her camera lens. "I'm so glad you invited me to come with you. I might have missed this."

She loved to hike—why hadn't she done more of it in the past year?

The answer to that was easy enough. Her former fiancé, Matt, hated to hike. They had gone together exactly once. He had huffed and puffed after her on a fairly moderate trail in Starved Rock State Park. "What about this, exactly, is supposed to be fun?" he'd gasped out when he reached the top of the hill where she was waiting.

"Check out this view." She'd gestured to the fall scenery spread out before them.

"I bet there are hundreds of pictures of this on-line," he'd said. "Even videos. All of which I could see without having to make that climb." He'd pulled a bottle of water from his pack, unscrewed the top and drunk deeply.

"You just need to get in better shape," she'd said, poking at his stomach, which had developed a bit of a paunch lately.

"Hey!" He'd drawn back. "I thought you liked my shape."

"I was just teasing," she'd said. "Of course I like your shape."

He had calmed down after that but had still made it clear he hadn't enjoyed the day, and they had never gone again. One more reason things probably would never have worked out for them.

"Hey, Roslyn, come on!"

She looked up to find the others a hundred feet ahead of her down the trail. "Coming!" she called, and started out after them. But she hadn't gone far before she veered off to take photos of a group of brilliant red paintbrushes. Everywhere she looked she spotted something else she wanted to capture.

Cheri trotted back to join her. "I don't mean to hold you up," Roslyn said. "I just keep seeing more flowers I want to photograph. I'm thinking I could frame a bunch of these photos for a gallery wall in my dining area."

"That would look great," Cheri said. "I never think of things like that."

"Cheri! Roz! We need to head back!"

Both women turned to see Buck waving from a couple hundred yards down the trail. Wes and Amber stood with him. Cheri returned the wave. "We're on our way!" she shouted. She glanced over her shoulder and frowned at the column of smoke rising over the ridge in front of them. "The smoke does look worse," she said. "I guess Buck's right and we'd better go."

"I'll catch up in just a minute," Roslyn said. "There's a thick patch of paintbrush up the slope a little that I want to get a shot of."

"I can wait for you," Cheri said.

"Don't be silly. I'll get the picture and catch up in no time. Go on."

"Cheri!" Buck shouted.

"Don't be too long," Cheri said, then turned and started back toward Buck and the others.

Smiling to herself, Roslyn hugged the camera to her chest and headed up the trail a little farther. The clump of flowers she wanted to photograph was just at the top of a rise to her left. The muted light from the smoke-filled skies really made the colors pop. She left the trail and picked her way through the thick grass and scattered rocks toward the blooms. At the top of the rise near the flowers she stopped to catch her breath. She definitely wasn't as nimble as she used to be. While she waited for her breathing to return to normal, she scanned the landscape before her. Not far from here the meadow ended at a rock outcropping shadowed by a thick growth of trees. Movement in the shadows attracted her attention and she shaded her eyes with one hand and squinted, hoping to spot an elk or other wild animal. She probably couldn't get a good photograph from here, but if she waited and it stepped into the light...

She shook her head and dropped her hand to her side. She didn't have time to wait for an animal to move into the perfect position for a photograph. She needed to get back to Cheri and the others. She turned toward the flowers and crouched to get a better shot. She took several photos, then shifted to focus on a butterfly perfectly positioned on a sun-flower. The light was perfect, the smoke in the air softening the harshness of the sun and lending depth to the colors.

While she was crouched down like this, she aimed her camera up the hill, toward the contrast of blue sky and dark smoke rising above the deep green trees and variegated gray of the rocks. With the right crop-ping, she might end up with a really moody land-scape.

A sudden noise, like someone—or something—scrambling over the rocks, startled her. She gasped and tried to stand, but she lost her balance and fell sideways, her feet sliding out from under her. She swore as a sharp pain lanced through her, bringing tears to her eyes. She managed to keep hold of the camera and rolled over into a sitting position, then stared down at her now-throbbing ankle. She tried to flex her foot and was rewarded with another sharp pain. "Ouch!" she cried out loud, and sat back once more.

She scowled at her foot, then leaned forward and

gingerly untied her hiking boot and felt her ankle. It was definitely swelling. Not broken, she hoped, but too sprained to go far. "Cheri!" she shouted, putting as much energy behind the cry as she could. "Buck! Help!"

She waited, holding her breath, but heard no answer. The wind had picked up and was blowing toward her, carrying her voice in the wrong direction.

She shifted again to remove her day pack. She stowed the camera inside the pack and slipped her cell phone from the side pocket. A message in the top left corner read No Service. If she could climb up on those rocks, she might be able to find a signal. She considered the challenge for a moment. If she was very careful, maybe she could walk. She moved forward, onto her knees, and tried to stand.

"Owww!" She howled in pain and crumpled as her foot refused to support her weight. Tears stinging her eyes, she eased into a sitting position again and considered her situation. Cheri and Buck would be worried when she didn't join them soon. They'd come back to find her, and they could help her limp down the trail. All she had to do was wait.

And hope that whatever she had heard up there in those rocks didn't decide to come down and investigate. An elk would probably leave her alone, but there were bears and mountain lions in the area. Maybe one of them had been displaced by the fire and was looking for a new place to live. And a meal.

She pushed the thought away and tried to focus on the beauty around her. She would be all right. All she had to do was wait for help. Patience wasn't exactly her strongest quality, but she had learned these last few months that there were plenty of things in life that you just couldn't rush.

DILLON WASTED THE rest of the morning on a fruitless internet search for Rosie. Plenty of people had advised him to let go of what was clearly becoming an obsession with the woman, but he couldn't get past this need to know why she had disappeared. If she really didn't want to see him again, he needed to hear it from her own lips.

He stared out the window of his home office, at the expanse of woodland in front of the home he had purchased the year before. Immediately after the weekend he and Rosie had spent together, he had imagined bringing her here. Would she see the same possibilities here, to make a home and a family? Or would she run away as fast as she could when she realized the direction his thoughts were taking? Even he didn't understand why he felt this way about her. He had been happy so far to date casually and have women as friends. No one had ever affected him the way Rosie had.

"What makes you happy?" she had asked. They had been lying in bed, drowsy and content after making love. She was good at asking questions that required more than one-word answers. Not nosy questions, exactly, but queries that made him think. And she seemed truly interested in his answers.

"My work makes me happy," he'd said. "I enjoy

my coworkers, but I also feel like I'm doing something important. I'm helping people."

"Police are supposed to help people, so that's good," she'd said. "What else? What else makes you happy?"

"My family makes me happy. They're good people. Fun to be with. And when we're together, I know they love me and will always love me, no matter what. It's what I want one day, with my own family."

"That's nice." She snuggled closer to him, so warm and soft. He couldn't remember being more comfortable and content.

"Your turn," he said. "What makes you happy?"

"Right now I'm happy," she said. "Just being here with you, in this perfect moment."

"What else?" he asked.

"That's enough." She kissed his shoulders, her lips soft, sending a tingle of awareness through him. "That's all I need."

The moment had been perfect, in a way. But he wanted more moments like that. More moments with her.

He straightened in his chair and picked up his phone. One more call, one he had been reluctant to make because it meant using his badge for what was, after all, a personal search. But he was getting desperate.

"Brundage Mountain Resort Grand Lodge. This is Susan. How may I help you?"

He introduced himself and explained that he was looking for a guest who had registered there five months before. She had introduced herself to him as Rosie Kenley. "But she might be going by another name. What I need from you is a list of all the female guests who stayed with you between February thirteenth and fifteenth of this year."

A long silence followed, so long he wondered if they had been disconnected. "Sir," Susan finally said. "You do know it's a holiday weekend, right? I'm here by myself and I've got a line of guests checking in. I can't possibly find that information for you now. I wouldn't even know how to find someone who stayed here five months ago. If you call back next Tuesday maybe somebody from our IT department can help you."

Dillon thanked her and ended the call. It had been a long shot, but he'd had to try. Bentley rose from his bed beside the desk and whined. "I know," Dillon said. "Time to quit sitting here and get moving. Want to go for a hike?"

Bentley let out an excited bark and trotted toward the mudroom, and the hook that held his leash. Dillon sat on a bench by the door and was lacing up his hiking boots when his phone rang again. This time the call was from Lieutenant Brady Nichols with Jasper Police. Was he calling to tell Dillon his day off was cut short?

"What's up, Brady?" Dillon answered the call.

"Corb Lund is playing in McCall next weekend. Cassie and I plan to go and wanted to see if you'd come along."

"I doubt if your girlfriend wants a third wheel on your date," Dillon said.

"You wouldn't be a third wheel. Cassie has a friend who wants to meet you, or you could invite someone."

"Thanks, but I'll pass," Dillon said. Ever since Brady had found the woman of his dreams in Cassie Whitaker, he'd been trying to help Dillon find his own happily-ever-after. It wasn't that Dillon was opposed to the idea of settling down—not at all. But he preferred to find his own women.

"Come on," Brady said. "It'll be fun."

Dillon's phone buzzed with an incoming text. He glanced down at the message: Lost hiker. We need you and Bentley at the Williams Gap Trailhead.

"I have go to, Brady," Dillon said. "I just got a text from Andrea. They need me to help find a lost hiker." Andrea Wayne, Mountaintop Search and Rescue Commander, would expect a prompt response to her summons.

"Good luck," Brady said. "But think about next weekend. It would be good for you to get out."

Yeah, he wouldn't mind going out next weekend, but with the right woman. One who captivated him as much as Rosie Kenley had. That was proving very hard to find. He stuffed the phone back in his pocket and grabbed Bentley's leash. "Change of plans," he said. "Are you ready to do some work?"

Half an hour later, Dillon and Bentley found Andrea and half a dozen other search and rescue volunteers gathered in front of the signboard for the trailhead, with two worried-looking couples. "Our friend, Roslyn Kern, was taking photographs of wildflowers," one of the young men, who introduced himself as Buck Teller, said. "She told us to go on and she would catch up. When she didn't show up after fifteen minutes, we went back to look for her but we couldn't find her."

"She couldn't just vanish, could she?" the young woman beside him asked. "Roslyn is so smart, and she's an experienced hiker."

"Even experienced hikers can get disoriented," Andrea said. "Do you have a photograph of Roslyn?"

Buck turned to the woman. "Cheri?"

Cheri paled. "I left my phone on the charger back at the hotel."

"Never mind," Andrea said. "Give us a description. How far up the trail did you last see her?"

"About two miles?" Buck said. "Something like that."

"Roslyn is about my height," Cheri said. "Five-six. With blond hair and green eyes. She's wearing jeans, a blue tunic top with lace, hiking boots, and she has a small day pack."

Andrea turned to Dillon. "This is Sergeant Dillon Diaz from the Jasper Police Department. He and his search dog, Bentley, are going to help look for your friend."

"Don't you need an item of clothing or something that belongs to Roslyn to do that?" Cheri asked. "I don't have anything like that."

"Bentley is trained to focus on the scent of any

person in the area and follow the scent trail to that person," Dillon said. "It would be helpful if you could tell us where you became separated from her."

"It was about two miles up the trail, I think," Buck said. "I know it was this kind of open area."

"She stayed back to take pictures of this big clump of flowers up the hill from the trail," Cheri said.

Dillon nodded. "That's helpful to know. It will give us a place to focus on."

Buck looked down at Bentley. "Doesn't he get confused, with so many people around?" he asked.

"Not usually." Dillon looked down at Bentley, who stared up at them with intelligent, alert eyes. It was difficult to explain to people who hadn't worked with dogs before just how good they could be at their jobs. "Bentley is young, but he's had good success so far. I can't guarantee we'll find your friend, but you did the right thing, not waiting to report her missing."

"The fire looks like it's getting worse." Cheri looked back toward the smoke that filled the sky behind them. "I'm worried she'll get caught in it."

"We're going to head out now," Dillon said. He shared Cheri's worries about the fire. In the last half hour the wind had shifted, pushing the flames—and a lot of smoke—in this direction.

"We'll have other groups of searchers farther back on the trail," Andrea said. "Radio if you determine a direction Ms. Kern is headed in."

"Roger that." Dillon started up the trail, moving quickly, Bentley on a leash at his side. When they

were away from the crowd at the trailhead, he unclipped Bentley's leash. "Ok, boy," he said. "Find."

Bentley pricked his ears and lifted his nose into
the air, then trotted forward, tail waving, ears alert.
Dillon moved on, setting a brisk pace. He didn't expect the dog to zero in on any one scent until they
were closer to the place where Cheri and Buck said
they had separated from Roslyn. A hot wind hit him
in the face, bringing the strong scent of wood smoke.
For a human, the mixture of aromas might be dis-
tracting, but Bentley had been trained to zero in on
the scent of people.

As part of Dillon's search and rescue training he
had taken a class that discussed the ways people
tended to behave when lost in the wilderness. The
patterns varied depending on a person's age, background and location but shared many similarities.
The majority of people, even those with experience
in the backcountry, tried to walk out on their own.
Roslyn's friends probably hadn't found her because
she had left the trail. In this country, with rapidly
changing elevations, stretches of open land inter-
spersed with woods, and barriers to travel such as
rock outcroppings and cliffs, it was easy for someone to disappear from sight even a few feet from an
established trail.

His phone buzzed with a new text. Before long,
he would be out of reach of a cell signal, but for now
he still had enough bars for reception. This one was
from Andrea: This is who you're looking for.

Dillon clicked on the attached photo and his heart

stumbled in its rhythm. Smiling up at him was a photo of Rosie Kenley—the woman he had been searching for for months.

He stared, heart racing, then his gaze shifted to the caption beneath the photo, which was from the website of a Chicago newspaper. "Rockin' Roz Kern greets fans at the annual WZPR Christmas bash."

Rockin' Roz? He scrolled further and found nothing. He tried a search on the name, but his signal was too weak. Bentley returned to his side and whined, the dog equivalent of "What's up? I thought we were looking for someone."

Dillon stuffed the phone back in his pocket. "Come on," he said to the dog. "Find Roslyn."

He moved faster now, the knowledge of who he was really looking for lending urgency to his steps. At the same time, he dreaded what he might find. Anger warred with longing. What did she mean, running out on him the way she had? What was up with the fake name? Had everything she had told him that weekend at Brundage been a lie? What was she doing here in Jasper?

And where was she now? Was she merely lost, or was she hurt? The idea made his stomach clench. "Roslyn!" he shouted, but the name only echoed back at him.

"Rrruff!" A bark from Bentley drew Dillon's attention. The dog stood, looking intently off trail. He glanced back at Dillon, tail wagging, and as soon as he saw that the man was following, the dog took off. He was running now, nose twitching and tail wagging. Ten yards up the trail, he veered off into the grass and picked up speed. Dillon jogged to keep up. "Roslyn!" he called again. "Roslyn Kern!" The name felt wrong on his tongue. His brain wanted to shout "Rosie!"

"Here I am! Over here!"

Dillon stopped and scanned the wildflower-strewn landscape for the source of the voice, but Bentley was already bounding up the hill. Dillon followed. He had to crest the ridge before he saw her, sitting almost hidden behind a tall clump of sunflowers. No wonder her friends hadn't spotted her. And they must never have gotten close enough for her to hear them calling for her.

Heart in his throat, he ran toward her. She was his Rosie all right—the same softly curved cheek and wavy golden hair. He couldn't see her eyes behind the sunglasses she wore, but he heard her gasp as he drew near. "Dillon!" she cried—though he couldn't tell if she was delighted to see him or merely shocked. She pushed up her sunglasses, as if to see him more clearly. "What are you doing here?"

"I'm looking for a lost hiker," he said. "You."

Bentley had stopped and sat beside her, tail thumping the ground. "Good boy!" Dillon said and scratched the dog's ears, then fished a chicken treat from his pocket and fed it to him.

"Is this Bentley?" Rosie—Roslyn—patted the dog. "I remember you talking about him, though I never thought he'd have to find me." She looked up and her eyes met his—a deep, clear green, and full of a mixture of emotions that mirrored his own—regret, curiosity and more than a little longing. "I'm sorry," she said. "I meant to get in touch with you before this, but things were so complicated when I got back to Chicago." She spread her hands wide in a gesture of surrender or helplessness—though he couldn't think of Rosie as helpless. One of the things that had drawn him to her was an impression of strength. She had been grieving the end of a relationship when they met, but she had been determined to get on with her life. He'd liked that about her.

"Never mind that now," he said. "Are you okay?"

She grimaced and looked down. For the first time he noticed she had taken off one of her hiking boots. "I think I sprained my ankle," she said. "A noise on the rocks up there startled me and I moved too fast and I guess I lost my balance." She sighed. "I figured the best thing to do was to stay here and wait for help. I thought my friends would come back to find me, but they must've been already too far ahead when they realized I wasn't going to be joining them."

"They did come back to look for you, but you somehow missed each other. They called 911 as soon as they were within cell phone range." He slipped off his pack and dropped it on the grass beside her, then knelt to examine her ankle.

"I'm really glad you came along when you did," she said. "The fire is looking a lot worse, and I wasn't sure how much longer I should stay here."

He glanced up at the sky, which had darkened with more smoke. "Let me take a look at that ankle," he said. He was grateful for something to do. Tending her injury would give him time to settle his emotions and figure out what to say to her.

She flinched when he took her foot in hand, but made no sound. He felt a shiver of desire as he stroked his hand across her instep and up to her ankle, and shoved aside the emotion. He was touching her in a professional capacity now, not as the lover he had been. "It's not too bad," he said. "I think if I wrap it tightly you could probably get your boot back on and I'll help you walk out. Or I could radio for a crew with a litter to carry you out."

"No! I'll walk! I hate to be so much trouble." She shifted as if prepared to stand up right then, but he laid a hand on her arm.

"Let me get this wrapped up first."

He fished first aid supplies from his pack, then radioed the commander. "I've found Roslyn," he said. "She has a sprained ankle, but it's not too bad. I think we can walk out, though you might send a couple of folks up the trail to meet us."

"Roger," Andrea said. "Hurry every chance you get. The wind is up and the fire is getting squirrelly."

"Understood. Ten-four." He stowed the radio once more and checked the sky. The wind was blowing smoke in their direction and Roslyn coughed, pulling his attention back to her. He took a bottle of water from his pack and handed it to her. "Drink this."

She took the bottle and twisted off the cap while he wrapped the foot in an elastic bandage. She said nothing, but he could feel her gaze on him, and his every nerve vibrated with awareness of her. All the times he had imagined them meeting again, he had never pictured a scenario like this, with her needing his help, forcing them into such intimacy.

He replaced her sock and helped her into her boot. She made a small noise of pain and he jerked his head up. "Are you okay?" he asked.

She relaxed her grimace. "I'm fine." She leaned forward and began to tie the laces of the boot. "I just want to get out of here." Their eyes met and she held his gaze. "Then you and I need to talk."

They had a lot of things they could talk about—but Dillon had no idea what he would say to her. His earlier anger had been overshadowed by his concern for her and the physical memory of how good they had been together. She finished lacing the boot and he bent to take her arm. "Lean on me all you want to," he said.

She nodded, and he pulled her to her feet and she leaned against him, pressed to his side. She felt different. Rounder. He glanced down and what he saw shook him, though he remained steady on his feet, still supporting her. She put a protective hand on her rounded belly. "That's what we need to talk about," she said. "I'm pregnant, and the baby is definitely yours."

Chapter Three

"Listen up, everyone." Jasper Chief of Police Doug Walters stood in the doorway of the department's squad room, a broad-shouldered man in his early sixties, with both the build and demeanor of a bulldog. He addressed the three officers gathered there: rookie Jason Wright, Lieutenant Brady Nichols and Officer Ava Callan. Brady, who had been texting with his girlfriend, Cassie, straightened and looked up at the chief, as did the others, including Ava's canine partner, a two-year-old German shepherd dog named Lacey.

"We've got a couple of urgent updates," Walters said in a voice that commanded attention. The chief had a no-nonsense approach to policing that could come across as gruff, but everyone under his command knew he had their backs. "The Gem Creek fire blew up in the last hour and headed east, toward Evans Ranch and the Skyline subdivision. We need every available officer out there going door-to-door to evacuate people and animals. The way the fire is headed, it could cut off the exit routes from those areas. Fire crews have requested we close Skyline Drive, County Road 16 and County Road 14 to all but local residents to clear the way for their personnel to get in and work on establishing fire breaks."

Adrenaline spiked through Brady as he imagined the scene near the fire. Though smoke-filled skies and heightened fire danger were a reality of summer in the West, having a big blaze practically in their backyard set everyone on edge. That kind of tension didn't bring out the best in some people.

"The Williams Gap Trailhead is on County Road 14," Ava said. "It's a pretty popular spot." A transplant from Chicago, Ava had been spending a lot of her off hours exploring local hiking trails with Lacey.

"If you see anyone there, tell them to leave," the chief said. "Otherwise, leave a notice on any vehicles parked there. We don't have time to look for hikers."

"Search and Rescue is already up there," Brady said. "I was talking to Dillon when he got the call to go out with Bentley to look for a lost hiker." He'd been hoping his invitation to hear some live music and meet Cassie's friend would get Dillon's mind off the mysterious Rosie, the weekend fling Dillon seemed obsessed with, but his friend hadn't seemed interested.

"He may have to call off the search if he's going to get out of there ahead of the fire," the chief said. "Focus on the homes in the area. Remind people that Daniels Canine Academy will take their dogs, and the animal shelter is open for other pets. They can move livestock to the fairgrounds in McCall."

"We've got better things to do than round up puppy dogs and horses," Captain Arthur Rutledge spoke from the doorway behind the chief. With thick, dark hair, brilliant blue eyes and a movie-star smile, the captain struck some people as being handsome and charming, but his coworkers in the police department weren't similarly impressed. Rutledge shouldered into the room, his expression grim. "This just came in from McCall PD." He handed the chief a piece of paper, then addressed the others. "Kent Anderson escaped from the South Boise Prison complex sometime last night. The PD in McCall contacted us because they received what they believe is a credible tip that Anderson was headed this way. He's apparently spent some time in the area and may have a hideout here."

Chief Walters looked up from the printout. "There's not much information to go on," he said. "Any idea who this 'credible tip' is from?"

Rutledge's suspiciously smooth forehead didn't crease, but the expression around his eyes tightened. "McCall PD thinks it's credible. That's enough for me. Anderson is a convicted mass murderer who's a danger to society. We should have every available officer out hunting for him."

"Hunt for him where, exactly?" Walters asked. "It's a big county and we don't have any information as to where he might be." He glanced at the others. "Everyone keep an eye out for anything suspicious while you're out and about. If you see anyone you think is Anderson, don't engage. Call for backup."

"Is Kent Anderson the guy who was convicted of the shooting on the Idaho State campus year before last?" Jason asked. The rookie had an eager energy that made Brady feel jaded sometimes.

"That's him," Captain Rutledge said. "He killed two prison guards when he escaped. I'm not going to give him a chance to get the jump on me."

"That's enough, Arthur," the chief said.

The captain faced the chief. "Instead of worrying about people who ought to have sense enough to evacuate without being told, we should be out hunting this fugitive," he said.

Nothing new here. The captain and the chief often disagreed about the best approach to policing. Their disagreements had only escalated since the chief announced his intention to retire soon. Rutledge, who as the most senior member of the force was the natural successor to Walters, seemed to believe he was already in charge.

"When we have a location, or even an area, to search, we'll do so," the chief said. "Until then, we have a duty to help our local citizens. Now get out there and do your job." He turned and left the room, leaving Rutledge staring after him.

The others stood and began gathering items, ready to head out. Rutledge glared at them a moment, then left. Moments later, the others followed.

Jason fell into step beside Brady. The young officer had grown up in the area and fit in well with the department. His recent engagement to his longtime girlfriend, veterinary assistant Tashya Pratt, had given him a new maturity. "What do we do if someone refuses to evacuate?" Jason asked as they headed down the hall toward the exit.

"We can't make them leave," Brady said. "Just remind them if the road gets cut off by the fire, no one will be able to come in and save them. If someone is adamant they don't want to go, ask about other family members or pets. Do they want to endanger them, too? Sometimes that works."

"And if it doesn't, they're on their own," Ava said as she and Lacey caught up with the two men at the employee entrance of the Jasper Police Department headquarters. "We do everything we can to help, but in the end, they're entitled to make their own decisions."

"I wonder if there's really anything to that tip about Kent Anderson being in the area," Brady said. "I never heard anything about him having a connection to Jasper. If he had, this place would have been crawling with reporters. The media was all over that story for months."

They exited into the parking lot and stood for a moment, continuing the conversation. "I was still in Chicago when the shooting at Idaho State went down," Ava said. "I didn't pay much attention to the details."

"Anderson was a graduate student at ISU," Brady said. "He had been removed from a teaching assistant position because of what university officials said was 'erratic behavior'. One April day he walked into his former class and shot and killed six people, including the professor."

"I remember," Jason said. "Didn't his defense team claim he had snapped because of the stress of exams?"

"They did," Brady said. "But the jury didn't buy it."

"Maybe the captain is right," Ava said. "And we should be focused on hunting him."

"Without more to go on than a tip that he was seen 'somewhere' near here, where would we even start?" Brady shook his head. "I'm all for going after the guy, but with the town full of tourists and a wildfire threatening, we're already spreading ourselves pretty thin."

"And Dillon is off trying to track down one of those tourists," Ava said. "Is it an adult or a kid?"

"An adult, I'm pretty sure," Brady said. "He said the text from the commander said a lost hiker, not a lost child. I think Andrea would have differentiated." A child at risk always added urgency to any mission.

"I've got to admit, I'm a little envious," Ava said. "I'd rather be out there working with my dog than knocking on doors telling people they need to leave their homes." She smiled down at Lacey, who returned the fond look and wagged her tail.

"If I hadn't been on duty today, Winnie and I would be out there," Brady said. The yellow lab loved nothing better than time in the woods, using that incredible nose of hers to find someone in trouble.

She and Dillon's dog, Bentley, had trained together. It was one of the things that had brought the two men closer.

"Let's hope Dillon and Bentley find whoever they're looking for and get back before the fire cuts them off." Ava glanced at the dark clouds of smoke in the distance. "In the city all I had to deal with were gangs and the occasional riot. When Mother Nature goes rogue, all you can do is get out of the way. Can't say I like that much."

"It's one of the trade-offs for living in such a beautiful place," Brady said. "When you're skiing on a blue-sky day in the backcountry this winter, you'll know it's worth it."

"Right." They moved farther into the parking lot and Ava opened the door of her cruiser. Lacey hopped into the back seat, graceful in spite of her ninety-pound bulk. "I'm going to stop at the trailhead on my way over to Skyline," Ava said. "If I see Dillon I'll give him a hard time about being off today and missing out on all the fun."

Brady shook his head and slid into the passenger seat of his own cruiser. The smell of smoke was stronger now, and a gust of wind sent ash drifting onto the hood of his vehicle. The fire was still some distance away, but things could change so quickly. Mother Nature was definitely going rogue. He'd feel better when his friend was back with them, dealing with more controllable things like unruly tourists or even fugitive killers.

STILL LEANING AGAINST DILLON, Roslyn studied his face, trying to gauge his reaction to her announcement about her pregnancy. She had hoped to work up to the subject more gradually, but this close together, there was no hiding her condition, so she'd blurted it out. His normally bronzed skin had blanched a shade paler and his hazel green eyes had widened, then he looked away, even as his arm around her tightened. "Come on," he said. "Let's see if you can walk."

She wanted to protest that they should stay and talk, but given the thickening smoke, that wouldn't be smart. And maybe the walk out would give him more time to digest this big upheaval in his life— and give her a little more space to think of what to say. She had so much to apologize for, and so much she needed to explain.

Gingerly, she eased her weight onto the wrapped ankle. A twinge of pain shot through her but soon subsided to a dull ache. "The bandage really helps," she said. She took a step forward, then eased her arm from around him. "I think I'm good. At least enough to get back to the trailhead."

"How are you feeling besides your ankle?" he asked. "I should have asked before."

"I'm fine." She glanced back at him. His gaze was focused on her midsection, so no sense avoiding talking about the baby altogether. "Now that I'm past my first trimester, I'm actually feeling great. My doctor says I have nothing to worry about."

"Hold up a minute." He put a hand on her arm, then took off his pack and dug in it. "I should have thought of this before." He held out a packaged mask. "All this smoke can't be good for you or the baby. This will help."

"Thanks." She opened the mask and slipped it on, then met his eyes once more.

"Why didn't you tell me about the baby before now?" he asked. "Were you planning to keep it a secret forever?"

She tried not to flinch at the anger behind his words. He had a right to be upset with her. But how could she explain that she had been reluctant to tell him about the baby because she feared the worst— another rejection from a man she had grown to care about? After all, she and Dillon had spent a single weekend together. Why should he welcome her turning his whole world upside down? "No! I came to Jasper this weekend specifically to find you and tell you." She smoothed her tunic over her belly, a habit she had developed of late, as if to reassure herself the baby was still there. Still all right. "As for why I didn't tell you before, it's complicated."

He moved up beside her on the trail. "We've got a long walk ahead of us," he said. "Why don't you start at the beginning?"

So much for waiting. Apparently, he didn't think he needed more time. But she felt far from ready. How many times in the last months had she antici-pated this conversation? She had rehearsed what she would say to him, and formulated defenses and ex-planations based on the various reactions she had imagined he might have. But now that she was here, with him so close she could smell the scent of his shampoo and feel the heat of his body beside her, all those planned words vanished. She glanced up at him, his jaw set in a firm line, his gaze directed outward. She sensed the hurt behind that stony expression and felt ashamed.

"I'm sorry," she said again. "I know I've messed this up. I was just..." She shook her head. No excuses. She had been dealing with a lot, but that didn't make up for the way she had treated a man who had been nothing but kind to her.

"Start with why you told me your name was Rosie Kenley," he said.

She nodded. "I told you the truth about why I came to Brundage Mountain that weekend," she said. "I broke up with my fiancé and lost my job and needed to get away and regroup. What I didn't tell you was that the man I was engaged to and I were the top-rated morning drive-time team on Chicago Radio. It was a very public breakup and a huge scandal. The local media wouldn't let up about it. The pressure was really getting to me."

"Rockin' Roz," Dillon said.

She stared at him. "You knew?" Come to think of it, he had addressed her by her real name when they had first met today. Had he known her identity all along and hadn't bothered to contact her?

"Not until today. The picture the search and rescue team received of you was from a newspaper in Chicago. The caption identified you as Rockin' Roz."

The hurt in his eyes wounded her. "I didn't use

my real name when I checked into the resort because I didn't want the Chicago media tracking me down. I can't even describe the way they hounded me." A clip of her fiancé, DJ Matt Judson, talking about their breakup had gone viral and for weeks she had dealt with reporters camped out in front of her condo building and photographers following her when she went to buy groceries or work out at the gym. It didn't help that within a few weeks of their split, Matt had started a new relationship with the woman who had replaced Roslyn on-air. He was quick to portray Roslyn as the cruel woman who had broken his heart, while his new love was the sweetheart who was going to heal his wounds.

"When I met you it seemed like a good idea to keep up the pretense," she said. "I didn't know you that well, after all. By the time we became closer, there was never a good time to reveal my real identity." Being someone else for a weekend had been such a relief—an escape from the mess she had made of her life.

"When did you find out you were pregnant?" he asked.

"Three months ago. I was shocked." She had burst into tears in the doctor's office, not her proudest moment. "I knew I had to tell you, I just needed time to figure out how. I didn't want to just call out of the blue. And I didn't have your number, anyway. I thought this was something that needed to be revealed in person, but I didn't know where you lived, only that you were an officer with the Jasper Police."

"You could have come looking for me three months ago," he said.

"Maybe I should have, but I was too scared."

He stopped, and she stopped, too. "You were scared of me?" He looked incredulous.

"I'd already been rejected, in front of hundreds of thousands of people, by the man I thought I would marry," she said. "I lost the job I loved." One day, she was on top of the world, the next it felt as if she had lost everything. How could she make Dillon understand the devastation of that experience? The baby had felt like one more obstacle to try to manage. She had had to pull herself together and find a way to not only support herself, but a child. She had to rebuild her reputation and her self-esteem. The idea of facing Dillon before she had pulled herself together had been too much. "Matt had made a big deal out of not wanting children," she added. "And he wasn't the first man I'd dated who talked about not wanting to be a father. What if you felt the same way? Maybe I'm a coward, but I couldn't face that." She hugged her arms across her stomach.

Some of the stiffness went out of his shoulders. "It's a lot to take in. I can understand that." He raked a hand through his short hair. "But you don't ever have to be afraid of me."

She blinked back sudden tears. Surely part of her had known that, or she might never have come to Jasper. The truth was, she had wanted to see Dillon again, to see if he was really as special as she remembered.

"The smoke is getting a lot worse," he said.

She started to answer, but a cough cut off her words. She looked around them, and was surprised to see that in the short time they had been walking and talking, the sky had darkened even more, with dense gray clouds boiling up over the mountain peaks. Her eyes stung from the smoke and as she gazed up at a ridge to their left, orange tongues of flame leaped up amid the black clouds. Fear lanced through her, and she gripped his arm more tightly. She wanted to ask him if they were in danger, but she couldn't form the words.

Dillon started to say something else, but his radio crackled. He unsnapped it from his belt and keyed it to receive. "What's your twenty?" a woman's voice asked.

"We've walked about half a mile on the trail, toward the trailhead," he said.

"The fire has crossed the trail near the base of Wilder Mesa." The woman's voice was pinched with agitation. "You'll need to cut across to the Cow Creek Loop and come back that way."

Dillon's forehead creased in a scowl. "Cow Creek Loop adds at least nine miles," he said. "Is there another route we can take?"

"Negative," the woman said. "The whole area under the mesa is active fire right now. The wind is blowing away from Williams Ridge and the loop follows Cow Creek for several miles, so that's an extra buffer."

"Ten-four," Dillon said and snapped the radio

back into its holder. He turned to meet Roslyn's worried gaze. "You heard?"

"Yes."

"How's your ankle?"

They both looked down at her bandaged foot.

"It's okay," she said. Throbbing a little, but she could deal with that. After all she had overcome in the last months, she wasn't going to let a wildfire defeat her. She drew in a deep breath, straightened her shoulders and looked him in the eye. "I guess we'd better start walking."

Chapter Four

The normally quiet grounds of Daniels Canine Academy resembled a cross between a dog show and a circus when Brady pulled up in his cruiser late Friday afternoon. Vehicles occupied every spot in the gravel lot and lined the driveway, and people and dogs milled about in every direction, agitated barks and excited shouts filling the air with sound.

Brady maneuvered his cruiser into a tight spot between a camper van and a one-ton pickup and turned to his passengers. "You two are going to behave for me, right?"

Two dogs—a "may have been a Lab" black mutt and a long-haired dachshund—panted at him, ears drawn back with anxiety. Brady leaned back and snapped on the leashes the owners had supplied, then went around to the back and retrieved the dogs. They jumped out and the black one—Billy—immediately lifted his leg on the back tire of the cruiser. The dachshund—Dolly—sniffed the ground with interest.

"Come on." Brady tugged on the leashes. "Let's see what Emma has set up."

He passed half a dozen people walking dogs on leashes as he made his way around to the kennel entrance. Some of them he recognized—others he didn't know. A few waved, and some of the dogs barked. Dolly let out a low growl, while Billy gamboled at the end of the leash like a kid on an outing to the zoo.

Brady pushed open the door to the kennels and was assaulted by even more noise and the mingled odors of dog hair, urine and kibble. People and dogs were lined up along the walls. At her desk, Barbara talked into the phone tucked between her shoulder and cheek and typed into the computer while a man in jeans and a Western shirt leaned over her desk, a pug cradled in his arms.

The man glanced at Brady and inched to the side. "Hello, Officer," he said.

"Hello, Tom." He recognized Tom Fletcher, from the feedstore in town. "Who do you have there?" He nodded to the pug.

"This is Denny." He shifted to give a better view of the dog. "I was in town when we got the word we needed to evacuate. My wife didn't know what to do, so she let one of the deputies take Denny to bring him here. Soon as I found out I came here to get him. We'll drive over to Riggins to stay with my sister until this is past, and she's got plenty of room to take Denny, too." He rubbed the dog's ears. "I'm grateful to Emma for taking in people's pets, but Denny will be happier with us."

"And you'll be happier, too," Brady said.

"That, too," Tom agreed.

Barbara set down the phone and looked up at them. "Thanks for waiting, Tom. Just sign here that you took charge of Denny and you can be on your way." She slid a clipboard toward him, then leaned over to look past Brady to the two dogs at his feet. "Who do you have for us, Brady?"

"This is Billy and Dolly. Their owner, Darlene Zapata, is taking her four kids to stay with her brother in McCall, but they needed a safe place for the dogs."

"Billy and Dolly Zapata," Barbara said as she typed, eyes on the computer screen. "Address and phone?"

Brady gave her the information and Kyle, one of the boys who worked for Emma, came to take the leashes. "I'll put them in a kennel together," he said. "They'll be okay."

"Thanks." Brady turned back to Barbara. "Looks like you've got a full house."

"And then some," she said. "But we're making room for everybody. Emma even has some of the smaller dogs up at her house. I'm making sure we keep track of everyone."

"Have you heard anything from Dillon?" Brady asked.

"No. Is he helping with evacuation?"

"No. He's off today. He and Bentley got called out

to look for a lost hiker. I was hoping he was done and had stopped by here."

"He was here for a few minutes this morning, but I haven't heard from him since. Sorry." She looked over his shoulder. "Can I help you?"

"The officer we talked to said we could bring Samson to stay while we're at the shelter," a woman said.

Brady turned and stifled a gasp as he faced one of the largest dogs he had ever seen. The petite brunette—she couldn't have weighed more than ninety pounds fully clothed—who was holding on to the leash smiled. "Samson is an English mastiff. He's big, but he's really a big baby."

Samson panted, tongue lolling, and regarded Brady with liquid brown eyes.

"Ma'am, can I get a shot of you and that humongous dog?" Both Brady and the woman turned to face a man with a shoulder-mounted video camera. "Officer, move over beside her, would you?"

A trim redhead in a purple sleeveless dress and low heels stepped out from behind the man and thrust a microphone toward Brady. "Officer, could you tell us how local law enforcement is handling the crisis brought on by the wildfire?"

Brady pushed the microphone aside. "Who are you?"

"Belle Fontaine, KBOI TV, Boise." She flashed a smile full of dazzling white teeth. "How are you dealing with the twin emergencies of an out-of-control wildfire and an escaped murderer in your charming, but tiny, town?"

Brady wanted to point out that the fire was not out-of-control, and demand to know how she had learned of the supposed sighting of Kent Anderson in Jasper, but his training held firm. "No comment," he said and turned away.

"I thought I told you people you need to leave. Now!" Emma had emerged from her office and made a beeline for Ms. Fontaine and her cameraman. "This is private property and you are not welcome here."

Belle Fontaine's smile never faded. "I'm sure our viewers will be very interested in the work you are doing to help local people and their pets," she said. "They'll probably be inspired to donate money to help Daniels Canine Academy with the important work I'm sure you do."

"I don't need your viewers' donations," Emma said. Her cheeks were flushed red, though the rest of her was pale. Brady had the impression of an overheated kettle about to blow. "I need you to leave."

Brady stepped forward. "You need to leave now, ma'am," he said. "This is private property and you're trespassing."

"I'm just trying to do my job," Belle protested. Her cameraman was already headed toward the door.

"So is Ms. Daniels," Brady said. "You need to leave her to do it."

He ushered her toward the door, then followed her and her cameraman all the way to their van. "What are you doing here?" Belle asked. "Why aren't you hunting for Kent Anderson?"

"How did you learn about Anderson?" Brady asked.

She sniffed. "I'm not obligated to reveal my sources."

And I'm not obligated to answer your questions, Brady thought but remained silent.

"We have a right to report this story," she said.

"Or course you do," Brady agreed. "As long as you stay on public property."

He waited until they had driven away, before he returned to the kennels, where he found Emma with the brunette and her dog. "Aren't you gorgeous?" Emma cooed to Samson.

"They're gone," Brady said. "Though I can't promise they won't come back after I leave."

"Thanks," Emma said. "And it's not that I have anything against press coverage of DCA, but it's just too crowded right now to have anyone here who isn't necessary."

"I'll take that as my cue to leave," Brady said.

"Thanks again," Emma said. "And thanks for helping people with their pets."

He waved and turned away. "I've got just the place for this boy," he heard Emma say as he left. "Do you know if he likes horses?"

"He loves horses. We have two of them," the woman said.

"Then he can have a kennel in the barn with my

two." Emma waved at Brady and led Samson and the brunette away.

He threaded his way once more through the mass of people and dogs, back to his cruiser. At the vehicle, he tried Dillon's phone. No answer. Then he called the PD. Teresa, the department secretary, answered. "Hello, Brady," she said. "I don't even have to ask where you are—I can hear the barking."

"Just checking to see if there's anything else for me before I call it a day," Brady said. "Any more news about Kent Anderson?"

"The chief was able to get a little more information from McCall. They received a report that Anderson hitched a ride from a man who dropped him off just north of the town limits," Teresa said. "That part checks out, but if anyone has seen him since, they haven't told us."

"Any word on that missing hiker Search and Rescue was looking for?" Brady asked.

"I believe she was found. But I don't know any more. My other line is ringing. Anything else?"

"No. That's it."

"Then get some rest. I imagine you'll be even busier tomorrow. We've got overflow crowds on the street and no telling what the fire will do overnight. It's guaranteed to be an exciting weekend, though whether the excitement is the good kind or the bad kind, it's too soon to tell."

Brady ended the call, then pulled up Dillon's number again. Where are you? he texted. You can't hide from the tourists forever.

DILLON WALKED BEHIND ROSLYN, back the way they had come. From behind, he couldn't even tell she was pregnant. With that loose top she was wearing, it hadn't been obvious when she was sitting down, either. Only when she had stood and leaned against him had he realized what he had missed before. Her announcement floated on the surface of his thoughts, refusing to sink in. A baby. *His* baby. He was going to be a father? He couldn't believe it.

He was still hurt that she hadn't confided in him sooner, but the anger he had nursed for months was quickly melting away. The distress in her voice when she had described her humiliating breakup and the harassment from the press afterward had cut through his own annoyance. And as much as he wished she had told him all of that in the beginning, she was right when she said they hadn't known each other that well. Yes, they had grown close in a very short time, but he could understand her feeling cautious about trusting another man again.

And now she was going to have a baby. His baby. His mom was going to be over the moon about this news. Colleen Diaz had made no secret of the fact that she thought she was overdue to be a grandmother. "Bentley is a wonderful dog, but he's no substitute for a grandchild," she had told him only last week. "I know you don't have any trouble attracting women. Can't you find one to settle down with? Someone who will make you happy and give me beautiful babies to spoil?"

He should probably hold off telling his mom about

Roslyn for a while. Colleen was warm and generous, but she could be a bit of a steamroller sometimes.

He shifted his attention to Roslyn once more and noticed she was favoring her injured ankle. "Hold on a minute," he said and hurried up to take her arm. "Let's find someplace to sit and rest a minute."

"But the fire." She looked around them, at the smoky skies.

"We're headed away from the fire," he said. "See, the wind is blowing away from us. The smoke isn't as heavy here as it was only a few minutes ago. We'll be okay."

He led her to a cluster of boulders beside the trail and settled her against one. "Sit here and let me check your ankle. It's hurting you, isn't it?"

"Just a little." Bentley hopped up to sit beside her.

Dillon had noticed how quick the dog was to not only find people, but to comfort them when they were upset. "He's a natural for search and rescue work," Emma had said during their initial training. "He would be a great therapy dog, too. Just naturally empathetic."

Roslyn smoothed her hand over the dog's black-and-white coat. "You sure are a sweetie," she said. He knew she was talking to the dog, but he felt the words in his gut, an echo of things they had said to each other so many months ago. He pushed the memories aside and knelt and unlaced her boot, then cupped his hand around her ankle.

"It's pretty swollen," he said. "It would be better if you could elevate and ice it."

"That will have to wait." Bentley hopped down and she slipped off her pack and her mask and took out a water bottle and drank.

"At least your boot comes up high enough to offer some good support." He replaced the hiking boot and tied the laces, then moved to sit beside her. Bentley sniffed through the grass nearby. "You should eat something," he said. He should have thought of that before. She would need a lot of calories to keep going.

"I've got a protein bar in here somewhere," she said, digging in the pack.

"Take this." He retrieved an energy gel from his pack, something search and rescue teams routinely carried to provide quick fuel to rescuers and the rescued alike.

Roslyn accepted the packet and looked at it doubtfully. "It's okay," he assured her. "It tastes pretty good, and it's an easy to digest source of calories."

"Okay. Thanks." She opened the packet and squeezed some into her mouth. "Not bad." Then she frowned. "You're not having anything?"

"I ate right before I set out." Only a small lie, but he wasn't very hungry, and he wanted to save as much food as he could for her. And the baby. If he kept reminding himself, maybe the child would become more real to him.

"How long is it going to take us to get back to town?" she asked.

"With this detour I don't think we can get back there before dark." Nine miles was a lot to hike in a single afternoon for a determined athlete who wasn't dealing with an injured ankle and a pregnancy. "We'll need to spend the night."

He watched her closely and saw the flicker of panic in her eyes, though she quickly pushed it aside. "That doesn't sound very comfortable," she said after a moment.

"It probably won't be, but we'll find some kind of shelter. I can filter water and I've got enough food that we won't starve, though it won't be the best meal you ever ate." He smiled, hoping to lighten the mood. While he was sure he could keep her safe, he wished he could do more to make her comfortable. And he would feel a lot better once a doctor had checked her out and reassured them both that she and the baby were okay.

"If I wasn't moving so slowly we could get back to town sooner," she said. "I'll try to walk faster."

"No. It's more important that you take care of yourself."

She looked amused. "I'm pregnant, not ill."

"You're pregnant and you have a sprained ankle and this is really rough terrain. How far along are you?" She had said, but he had been so stunned that the information hadn't registered.

She laughed. "Do the math, Dillon."

Right. They had been together five months ago. Four months until he would be a father. He broke out in a cold sweat at the thought.

She laughed again. "What's so funny?" he asked.

"You. The tough, charming cop thrown for a

loop." Her expression sobered and she laid a hand on his arm. "I'm sorry. I know you didn't ask for this, and the way I sprung it on you was a little rough. I understand if you don't want to be involved."

"No." He grabbed her hand and held it when she tried to pull away. "I mean, yes, it's a surprise, but I'm not going to bail on my own kid. I just… I need a little time to wrap my head around this."

"I understand," she said. "I was pretty stunned when I first found out, too. I mean, I thought we were being careful."

"We were. Most of the time. But there was that one early morning…" They'd just awakened, warm in each other's arms, moving together still half asleep but so drawn to each other. No talking, only touching. Enjoying. Both knowing they wouldn't have much longer together.

Her cheeks flushed, and he thought she was probably remembering those moments also. She brought their still linked hands to rest on the small mound of her belly. "Do you feel that?" she whispered.

"Feel what?" But then the sensation of movement beneath their clasped hands startled him. He freed his fingers from hers and laid his palm flat against her, a rush of wonder going through him. "Is that the baby?"

"Yes." Their eyes met and hers were shiny with tears, though she was smiling.

A storm of emotion threatened to undo him—awe, fear and a rush of incredible tenderness. His palm still resting on her belly, he brought his free hand up to cradle the side of her face and brought his lips to hers. She stilled, and he started to pull away, then she leaned in, her mouth moving against his, the velvet brush of her lips reawakening old memories and kindling new passion. She angled her body toward his, and he slid his hand down the line of her neck and across her shoulders. How many nights since February had he dreamed of her in his arms again? Those dreams had kept him searching for her, long after a more sensible man would have accepted that she had rejected him.

This didn't feel like a rejection now.

"Ruff!"

Bentley's sharp bark jolted them apart. Dillon turned his head to see the dog at attention, body stiff, ears forward, staring intently toward a cluster of trees a hundred feet off the trail.

"What is it?" Roslyn asked. "Why is he acting like that?"

"I think someone is out there." He stood. "Maybe someone is following us."

Chapter Five

In a flash, Dillon had transformed from tender lover to this colder, harder version of himself. Like his dog, he was completely focused on whatever was in the woods out there, automatically positioning himself between her and possible harm, every nerve alert to danger. "Why would someone be following us?" she asked, the words pinched off and strained.

"I don't know." He checked the dog again. Bentley remained rigid, leaning toward whatever had caught his attention.

"Maybe it's an animal," Roslyn said. "They're probably trying to get away from the fire, too."

He didn't take his eyes off that line of trees. "Bentley tends to be pretty cautious around dangerous animals such as mountain lions or bears," he said. "The few times we've come across something like that while we're out hiking, he's stayed quiet and right by my side. This alert is more like when he finds someone he's been tracking—but different, too." He frowned.

"Different how?" she asked.

"More cautious."

His words sent a shiver up her spine. "As if whatever out there is dangerous," she said, her voice just above a whisper. She squinted, trying to make out anything in the shadows, but she saw nothing.

"Hello!" Dillon shouted. "Is anyone there?"

She held her breath, waiting, but only ringing silence answered.

"Bentley, find," Dillon commanded.

The dog looked up, eyes questioning, then sniffed the air and took a few tentative steps forward. He sniffed again, moved forward a few more steps, then stopped and sat. He looked back at Dillon, clearly asking what he should do next.

Dillon glanced toward the woods once more. "Whatever was out there must have moved on," he said.

"Do you really think someone is following us?" she asked.

"You were probably right about it being an animal."

She was about to point out that he had already told her Bentley wasn't reacting the way he did to an animal, but Dillon slipped on his pack and fastened the chest strap. "Are you ready to go?" he asked.

"Of course." She stood and settled her own pack. As far as she was concerned, the sooner they moved on, the better.

Dillon was staring at the line of trees again. "I want to walk up there and see if I spot anything," he said. "You can wait here."

"I'll go with you." The idea of being separated from him—especially if someone really was after them—unsettled her.

They started out across open ground toward the woods. They hadn't traveled far on the uneven ground before her ankle began to throb again. She focused on Dillon's back, determined to ignore the discomfort. She would have plenty of time to rest once they were safe. And Dillon was freaked out enough about her pregnancy without her adding to his fears. He did a pretty good job of masking his emotions regarding the baby, but she recognized the panic behind his surprise and awe.

She had felt that same awe when she had stared at the results of that first pregnancy test. She had even taken two more tests, sure that the first one must have been wrong. Even when she saw her doctor and he confirmed that she was indeed pregnant, it had been days before it felt real to her. She had even forgotten about the baby a few times until she began to feel him or her inside her. Though her doctor had offered the opportunity to learn the gender of the baby, she had declined. Everything about this baby had been a surprise, so why not one more?

Dillon moved much faster than she could up the slight slope toward the trees, the dog trotting in front of him. He made a striking figure, tall and muscular, long strides easily conquering the terrain. She had noticed him in the lift line that day at Brundage even before they loaded onto the same chair, but his easy charm and sense of humor had captivated her.

Add intelligence and an all-around sexy vibe, and he had been the perfect distraction to take her mind off her troubles.

But she apparently wasn't cut out for the kind of fling she could easily walk away from. Even before she had discovered she was pregnant, she had thought longingly of Dillon Diaz. She had daydreamed about going to Jasper and looking for him, to see if they could manage a long-distance relationship. But trying to juggle that along with rebuilding her career and regaining her confidence had been too daunting.

Now that she was here, though, and he wasn't running in the other direction from her and the baby, her old daydreams of being with him were quickly resurfacing. And that kiss…it had been unexpected, but definitely not unwelcome. Did it mean he was interested in something more, too? She hadn't dared to allow herself the fantasy of the two of them raising their baby together, but obviously that hope had been in the back of her mind all along, since it came rushing up to fill her thoughts now.

They reached the wooded area and Bentley raced around, barking and tail wagging. "That's the way he acted when he found me," she said.

Dillon didn't answer, his attention focused on the loose duff beneath the trees. "Do you see anything?" she asked, when she could stand the silence no longer.

"No." He turned back toward the trail. "Let's go. We need to find a safe place to spend the night."

They had been so close for a few moments there, but now he felt distant again. Was it because of this mysterious, unknown intruder, or because of something else? She searched for some topic of conversation to bring him back to her. "What have you been up to since February?" she asked. "Are you still with the police department?"

He straightened his shoulders and turned toward her. Not as open as he had been in the moments before he kissed her, but making an effort to be warmer. "I am," he said. "And I was pretty busy with search and rescue this past winter and spring. And I've been working with Bentley. I'm thinking of training him for wilderness rescue."

"How is that different from what you already do?" she asked. This was the wilderness, wasn't it?

"Right now, Bentley is trained as a tracking dog," Dillon said. At the sound of his name, Bentley looked over his shoulder at them. "He finds people by following their scent in the air. He's able to follow the scent someone leaves as he or she moves across an area and distinguish that aroma from smoke or plants or animals. He can follow the trail for miles. Wilderness tracking takes that talent for scent detection and hones it for rougher terrain and longer distances. That kind of work also requires more endurance, to travel over rougher terrain in varying conditions."

She nodded. It was interesting, but not what she most wanted to know right now. "Are you dating anyone?" she asked. Did he have a girlfriend? A fiancée? Someone who would definitely complicate any attempt to have a relationship that extended beyond their shared child?

"No."

Just—no. Without elaboration. She bit her tongue, sensing she shouldn't probe further. But what was this gorgeous, smart, gainfully employed and genuinely nice guy doing single? He clearly liked women and probably had half the women in town drooling over him. Was she really, really lucky, or was he really, really good at avoiding commitment?

"What about you?" he asked. "Did you get a job with another radio station?"

"No." She had put out a few tentative feelers, but after a couple of hints that she was too "controversial," followed by advice that she wait for the scandal to die down before she submitted any more applications, she had been fearful of ever being on-air again. "I started my own business," she said. "I do voiceovers for commercials and television. And I record audiobooks." She had spent years training for radio work and reasoned those skills would translate well to other voice work. Plus, she had experience doing commercials as part of her radio gig.

"Do you like the work?"

"I do. It's very different from what I did before, but I really like it. And I can set my own schedule, which will work well after the baby is born."

"Do you know if you're having a boy or a girl?" he asked.

"Not yet. I thought it might be nice to be surprised. But I'm scheduled for an ultrasound when I get back to Chicago. The doctor says I should be able to find out then, if I've changed my mind, though I don't think I will." She started to tell him he was welcome to attend the test with her, but that seemed like too much, too soon. Would he think she was pressuring him to be more involved than he wanted to be? He had a job and a life here in Jasper. She had no right to pull him out of that.

"How's the ankle?" he asked.

The change in topic made her wonder if talk of the baby was making him uncomfortable. She reminded herself once more that he hadn't had as much time to get used to the idea as she had. "It's okay." She was almost accustomed to the pain. "It's not getting any worse. I'll be fine." She looked around them. The trail had climbed and was following the top of a ridge now. As Dillon had promised, they had moved away from much of the smoke, though dark clouds on the horizon cast the landscape in twilight hues until it resembled a charcoal drawing. "Do you have any idea where we'll spend the night?" she asked.

"There are some caves a couple of miles ahead. They'll make a good shelter. We can make a fire, spread some pine boughs to sleep on." He looked back at her. "It won't be a posh hotel, but it won't be so bad."

Was he thinking of the very nice hotel where they had spent the weekend together all those months ago? That time seemed so long ago now, but in many ways like only last week. He was easy to be with, though she still didn't feel she knew him well. She would have to trust him, though. He was her best chance of getting herself and her baby to safety.

BRADY WAS ON his way back to his cabin when dispatch radioed for him to report to the station. He arrived to find the station crowded with officers, the assistant fire chief, and the search and rescue commander. "What's going on?" he asked Lieutenant Cal Hoover, who stood in the doorway of the squad room.

Cal's normally affable, dark face was creased with worry, making him look older than his forty-nine years. "I think we have a situation," he said. "The chief will fill in the details."

Brady followed him into the squad room and stood along the back wall, next to Jason. "I saw a television news van in town this afternoon," Jason said. "Think this has anything to do with them?"

"Maybe," Brady said. "A reporter and cameraman were out at DCA, trying to interview Emma."

"I bet that went over big," Jason said.

"She sent them packing. I told them they were free to do their job as long as they did it on public property."

"Are they here because of the fire, or because of Kent Anderson?" Jason asked.

"Both, I think," Brady said.

They fell silent as the chief entered the room, followed by Rich Newcomb, assistant fire chief, and SAR Commander Andrea Wayne. "Some of you already know that Sergeant Dillon Diaz isn't here because he and his search dog, Bentley, were called out this afternoon to look for a lost hiker," Chief Walters said. "I called you all here to fill you in on the newest development with that situation."

Brady's stomach dropped, and he exchanged anxious looks with several others around him. Had something happened to Dillon?

"Dillon and Bentley located the missing hiker, Roslyn Kern," Andrea said. "But before they could make their way back to the trailhead, the fire shifted and crossed the trail ahead of them. Thick smoke made visibility difficult, and the trail being blocked led me to direct the two of them to backtrack and head farther north and west to stay out of danger. Unfortunately, that put them out of cell phone and radio range, though we have no reason to believe they're in any trouble. During our last communication, Dillon reported that Ms. Kern had a sprained ankle but was capable of walking with his assistance. The friends who were hiking with Ms. Kern and reported her missing are fine, but apparently they've been talking to the reporters in town." Andrea looked to the chief, who took up the story.

"Roslyn Kern is from Chicago," Walters said. "Where, apparently, she was a very popular radio disc jockey and was involved in some kind of scandal. Among other things, she's pregnant. About five months, according to her friends."

"They should have mentioned her pregnancy when they first reported her missing," Ava said.

"Apparently, they were trying to honor her wishes

to keep the pregnancy private," Walters said. "In any case, when the reporters heard Kern's name, and that she was trapped by the fire—their words, not mine—they latched on to the story and ran with it. National news picked it up and media is descending on the town, searching for every angle they can find about the fire and Ms. Kern. Not to mention Kent Anderson."

"If they can find a way to link those three things, I guarantee they will," Captain Rutledge said.

Walters nodded. "Reporters have learned that Ms. Kern is with Sergeant Diaz, and they're playing that up in their stories as well. As you're carrying out your duties this weekend, you're probably going to be asked about Dillon, the fire, Kent Anderson, or all of the above. This is your official notice that your only reply is 'No comment.'"

"Have there been any more sightings of Anderson?" Cal asked.

"This afternoon I interviewed the driver who gave a ride to a man who fits Anderson's description," Rutledge said. "He seemed credible, though we can't know for sure. He said the man he later realized might be Anderson told him he was meeting friends in the area, and he seemed jumpy."

"How does he know the guy was Anderson?" Lieutenant Margaret Avery asked.

"He said he saw a news bulletin about Anderson's escape and recognized him."

"Where did he drop off this hitchhiker?" Jason asked.

"He says the guy asked to be let out at the intersection of County Road 14 and North Maple. The guy told him friends would pick him up there. The man he let out was wearing khaki trousers and a faded black T-shirt advertising a landscape service in McCall. McCall police think those items of clothing might have been taken from a clothesline in a backyard in town."

"That intersection isn't far from the Williams Gap Trailhead," Brady said.

"That information is definitely not to be shared with the media," Walters said.

"We didn't see anyone else up there when we were looking for Ms. Kern," Andrea said. "And her friends said they hadn't seen anyone else on the trail, either."

"We don't know for sure this hitchhiker was Anderson," Margaret said.

"We have to operate on the assumption that it was," Walters said. He turned to Newcomb. "Now I'd like the chief to update us on the latest situation with the Gem Creek fire."

Newcomb, a muscular man in his forties with a blond buzz cut, stepped forward and turned toward the map of the area that was tacked to the wall behind him. "This afternoon the fire grew to twelve thousand acres," he said. "To the east of Jasper, primarily on public land, though the Lazy H ranch lost a corral and a couple of outbuildings. Fire crews are establishing a line of defense that runs from here to here." He indicated two points on the map. "That's directly behind the Skyline development. Those homes have been evacuated as a precaution, and we have crews patrolling that area for any fire activity. The wind has decreased somewhat this afternoon, allowing us to gain some ground. Overnight, temperatures should cool, which should allow for more containment, and the forecast is calling for cloudy conditions in the morning, though whether or not that pans out we don't know. We're calling it twenty percent contained at this point."

Brady studied the map and tried to picture the location of the trail Dillon and Ms. Kern would follow to get back to town. It looked like they were away from the immediate path of the fire.

"As you all should know, wildfires are unpredictable," Newcomb continued. "There's a lot of fuel in the national forest around us. But we have at least one slurry bomber dedicated to this blaze, and a crew of smoke jumpers from Pinedale arrived this afternoon, so we're optimistic we can bring this under control. We're asking for your help keeping unauthorized persons out of the evacuation areas, or areas with active fire. Depending on how things play out, we may need to evacuate more houses."

"What about Dillon?" Ava asked. "Is there anything we can do to help him?"

"We're hopeful he'll move back into radio or cell phone range before long," Andrea said. "Given that Ms. Kern is injured and probably traveling slowly, I don't expect them to make it back to town before sometime tomorrow. I've asked the pilots of the spotter planes who are regularly surveying the burn area to keep an eye out for them. Right now, that's all we can do."

"Are the spotters looking for Kent Anderson, too?" Rutledge asked.

"They are," Walters answered. "They look for anyone down there who shouldn't be."

"What happens if they spot someone?" Cal asked. "Can we go in after them?"

"That depends on where they are and what they're doing," Walters said.

"We haven't had reports of any campers or hikers in the area who are unaccounted for," Newcomb said. "Though there's always the possibility of a lone backpacker or hiker who didn't register at the trailhead. If someone is in distress, we try to help them, but we can't put our volunteers in danger to do so."

"The trails in that area are well-marked," Walters said. "If they can get to a trail, they should be able to follow it out."

"Unless they don't want to leave," Rutledge said.

"Why wouldn't they want to leave?" Jason asked.

"I can't think of a better place to hide than the national forest," Rutledge said. "Especially if a wildfire is keeping authorities from getting to you. Anderson is supposedly familiar with the area. He may intend to travel deeper into the wilderness, where he could make his way down to Boise. Or he could head north, toward Canada."

"That's taking a big risk," Ava said.

"He's doing a life sentence," Rutledge said. "Maybe he feels he has nothing to lose."

"Any more questions?" Walters asked.

There were none, so he dismissed them. Brady pulled out his phone. Still no answer from Dillon. He texted Cassie to let her know he was on his way home, then for the second time that day emerged into a crowd of people, only this time without the dogs. "Officer, what can you tell us about the search for Roz Kern?" A tall man in a white shirt and blue tie thrust a microphone into his face.

"What can you tell us about Sergeant Diaz?" a woman, also with a microphone, asked.

"No comment," Brady said. He put his head down and headed toward his vehicle, which, unfortunately, was parked at the far end of the lot.

"Have you heard from Sergeant Diaz?" someone else asked—Brady didn't look up to see who. "Are he and Ms. Kern in danger from the fire?"

"How badly is Ms. Kern injured?"

"Do they know Kent Anderson is in the same area? Are they aware he could be stalking them?"

Brady did look up then, and zeroed in on the older man with heavy jowls who had asked the question. "What makes you think Anderson is stalking anyone?" he asked.

The reporter looked smug. "Anderson made it clear at his trial that he doesn't like lawmen. He swore to kill as many cops as he could. If he spots your friend out there alone with no backup, he probably won't pass up the chance to take him out."

Brady bit back a reply. Dillon wasn't in uniform, so how would Anderson know he was a cop? People said other cops and people who had spent a lot of time around law enforcement—like criminals—could always tell, but was that true? And the chance of Dillon and Anderson crossing paths seemed pretty remote. Still, the reporter's questions, and his attitude, angered Brady. Which he supposed was the point. He took a deep breath and looked the man in the eyes. "No comment," he said and continued toward his truck. To think he had who knew how many more days of dealing with this. *Hurry back anytime you can, Dillon,* he thought.

Chapter Six

As they continued along the trail, Dillon kept a watchful eye for signs that someone was following them. He hadn't said anything to Roslyn, but he knew Bentley wouldn't have alerted that way if someone hadn't been there. He had worked with the dog long enough that Dillon trusted him to be right. And hadn't Roslyn mentioned that she had sprained her ankle when she had been startled by the sound of someone in the woods? It might have been an animal, or even the wind in the trees, but what if it wasn't?

The shadows had lengthened and the sun wasn't as intense as it had been earlier in the day. They'd be out of light as soon as it dropped below the ridge to the west. Roslyn was sinking too; her shoulders slumped and her limp was more pronounced. She hadn't complained, but he knew she needed rest. The first aid course he had taken as part of his search and rescue training hadn't said much about special precautions for pregnant women, but he couldn't help thinking Roslyn's condition made her more vulnerable.

"The caves are just a little farther," he said.

"That's good." They were climbing and she sounded out of breath.

"Do you want to stop and rest a minute?" he asked.

"No. I'll rest when we get to wherever we're going to spend the night. When I stop, I don't plan to get up for a while."

That was Roslyn, quick-witted and cheerful whether faced with a long lift line or a night in the wilderness. He was sure she had her moments of despair—he hadn't missed the sadness in her voice when she had talked about her breakup and her job loss. But she was the type of person who worked to get past any setbacks and move forward with a positive attitude. That took a special strength he couldn't help but admire.

They entered a grove of aspens, the temperature dropping perceptively in the shade, the smell of damp leaf mold cutting through the faint tinge of smoke that clung to their clothing and hair. Their footsteps echoed as they crossed a footbridge over a small creek. "The caves are up here, overlooking the creek," he said and moved ahead of her to lead the way. The creek itself had slowed to a trickle in these dry months, but there were still a couple of pools where he could collect water to filter.

He hadn't hiked this trail in a couple of years, but the route was well-worn and easy to follow. The caves were a series of shallow openings carved into the rock over centuries. He led the way to the deepest one, which provided a space about eight feet deep and a little over five feet tall. Roslyn could stand upright, but he had to duck. A fire ring, the coals long grown cold, was arranged just inside the opening to the shelter. "This looks like a popular place," Roslyn said, looking around at the smooth stone walls and several large logs arranged as seating around the fire ring.

"Backpackers use this as an overnight spot sometimes," he said. The wildfire had probably sent everyone out of the area, so they had the campsite to themselves. "It's not deluxe, but we'll have shelter here." He touched her shoulder and she turned toward him. He could read the fatigue in her eyes and was glad they had stopped before dark. "I'm going to get some water and firewood. Will you be okay here by yourself?"

"Of course." She slipped off the mask and lowered herself to one of the log seats. If her smile was forced, at least she was making an effort. "I'll be fine."

He didn't like to leave her alone, but Bentley hadn't alerted to anyone near them since they had reached the ridge top, and it would be difficult for someone to sneak up on her as long as she stayed in the cave. He could have asked Bentley to stay with her, but the dog had already set out ahead of him. Dillon retraced their footsteps along the trail, but instead of heading down toward the creek, he first climbed up to a point that gave him a view of the surrounding area. Bentley turned and followed him, and sat by Dillon's side as he scanned the treed area along the creek, as well as the more open fields beyond. He saw nothing amiss. No other people, or any sign that anyone had passed this way in a while. The wind continued to blow away from them, clearing most of the smoke, though the valley below was still hazy. He watched a long time but saw no movement.

He tried his radio but raised only static. No surprise—they were a long way from a tower or a repeater. He didn't expect any better result from his phone, but when he took it out he was surprised to see a single bar of signal, flickering in and out. It wasn't enough to make a call, but he might be able to send a text. And at some point in their journey he had passed through an area where he was able to receive a text from Brady. You can't hide from the tourists forever, Brady had written.

Dillon hit the reply button. We stopped for the night at the caves above Cow Creek. Hold down the fort until we make it back tomorrow. He paused, his finger hovering over the screen. Part of him wanted to share the news that he had found the elusive Rosie—and that he was going to be a father in about four months. But the information still felt too raw and precious to expose to the public, even someone as nonjudgmental as Brady.

He hit Send, waited to make sure the message went through, then shut off the phone to conserve the battery, which had already drained to 40 percent. Then he headed back down to the creek to filter a couple of bottles of water. He would gather some

firewood to boil water for hot drinks and to cook the
freeze-dried meals that were part of his emergency
rations. He could cut some pine boughs, too. He had
never actually slept on pine boughs before, but he
had a vague memory of reading about wilderness
explorers sleeping on them, and they sounded more
comfortable than the hard rock floor of the cave. Tomorrow he and Roslyn would walk out to safety, but
for now his goal was to get through the night with
as little trauma as possible.

ROSLYN FELT GUILTY sitting while Dillon worked, so
after a while she shoved to her feet. She found a broken tree branch and used it to sweep the dirt floor of
the cave, sending dried leaves, loose rock and coals
from long-ago campfires over the edge toward the
creek below. She straightened the arrangement of
logs around the firepit, then looked for anything else
to do. There was nothing, so she settled onto a log
once more to wait.

Hunger gnawed at her like a wild animal. This
sudden desperate need to eat was only one of the
many things that surprised her about her pregnancy.
She dug in her pack for the protein bar and ate it
quickly. She felt only a little guilty about not waiting
for Dillon. He was probably hungry, too. He hadn't
eaten all day. But he had said he had plenty of pro-
visions in his pack.

She washed the bar down with the last of the water
in her bottle, then inventoried the rest of the contents
of the day pack. She had one of those foil blankets

that were supposed to keep you warm by reflecting body heat. That would probably come in handy tonight. Another protein bar, and some water purification tablets in a small brown bottle. A first aid kit that contained bandages, ibuprofen and antibiotic ointment, a roll of gauze, some tape and a pair of tweezers. A tin of matches. A whistle. A small mirror for signaling. All the things a person was supposed to carry hiking, though they hadn't helped her much today.

She took out the camera and turned it on to scroll through the photos on the memory card—not the pictures she had taken today, but photos from her weekend with Dillon in February. A shot of him next to her on the chairlift, only his grin recognizable beneath the helmet and goggles. A selfie of the two of them at the top of the mountain, goggles pushed up on top of their helmets, leaning in close with shoulders touching, a snow-covered peak rising behind them. Another photo of Dillon, this time seated across from her at dinner, freshly showered and shaved and wearing a black sweater, so handsome he had taken her breath away when they met up at the restaurant.

She had more images of him in her mind—walking arm in arm across the snowy parking lot to her hotel room, naked beside her in bed, sleepy-eyed with the shadow of a beard on his jaw as he sat across the breakfast table from her the next morning. Those pictures had occupied her more than she cared to admit in the months since she and Dillon had been together.

She had told herself she was so attracted to him then because he was such a change from Matt. Dillon had no expectations that she behave a certain way. Matt had choreographed every aspect of their relationship from the very beginning, as if writing a script for an on-air skit. She hadn't seen it that way at the time, of course. When he suggested she say a certain thing on air or wear a certain outfit when they appeared together, he had somehow made it seem as if they were brainstorming ideas together. Except the only ideas that ever developed into reality were his.

Dillon listened more than he spoke, and he didn't argue when her ideas or beliefs didn't match up with his. He seemed interested in what she had to say and trusted her to make her own decisions. In these last few hours she had spent with him she had felt the old attraction all over again but intensified. Maybe she was drawn to him not because he wasn't Matt, but because of what he was. The kind of man worth knowing better.

The sound of something approaching on the path made her heart beat faster. She stood in time to see him climbing up the trail with an armload of firewood. He dumped the wood beside the fire ring, then left again and returned shortly, dragging in a pile of pine branches. "Bedding," he said by way of explanation. He slipped off his pack and set two bottles of water beside the firewood, then unzipped a pocket and took out a packet she recognized as a foil emergency blanket.

"I have one of those in my pack," she said.

"Great. I'm thinking we can spread them over the boughs and maybe it will be better than sleeping on the ground."

She nodded. She had been dreading trying to get any rest on the hard rock. As it was, so much of her body ached she didn't think the few ibuprofen in her pack were going to do much good. And her doctor had recommended she avoid painkillers if possible.

Dillon shook out the blanket and let it drift down over the pile of branches, then regarded it critically. "It looks kind of lumpy," he said. "Want to try it out?"

She had her doubts but knelt and crawled onto the makeshift bed, the blanket crackling beneath her. She lay back, then squirmed until she settled into an almost comfortable position. "It's better than I thought it would be," she said. A little noisy. She sniffed. "And it smells good." Fresh and woodsy. Much better than the musky cave.

"That's about the best we can do," he said. He settled onto one of the logs and pulled his pack over. "You must be starving," he said. "I am."

"I ate a protein bar." She sat beside him, the pack between them. "Sorry, but I couldn't wait."

"It's okay." He pulled out a couple of foil pouches. "I've got chicken and noodles or lasagna," he said.

"The chicken." She didn't want to think about the heartburn the lasagna was liable to give her.

"There's hot chocolate and instant coffee, too. And some tea. Don't know what kind." He held up a handful of packets.

"Chocolate, please. You come well prepared."

"We never know how long we're going to be out on a search and rescue mission, or who we might need to feed in addition to ourselves, so we always carry some basics." He pulled out a small pot, unfolded handles from the side and poured water from one of the bottles into it. He set this aside, then leaned forward and began arranging wood in the fire circle. "I take it you didn't plan on being out very long today?"

"You mean because of the little pack I was carrying?" she asked.

"Your boots look pretty broken in," he said. "And I remember we talked about hiking in the area back in February, so I figured you would be better prepared for a long hike."

"This was kind of a last-minute outing," she said. "I ran into my friends Cheri and Buck in a café in town this morning. They're from Chicago, too, and came out for the holiday weekend. They were with another couple I didn't know, but they asked me to go hiking with them. Everyone had assured us there was no immediate danger from the wildfire, so I figured, why not? It was a beautiful day and I hoped I could get some good photographs of the wildflowers."

"I remember you took a lot of photographs at the ski resort," he said. "Is photography a passion of yours?"

"Sort of. I'm trying to improve. I've taken a few classes, but nothing serious. It's a good creative outlet. Anyway, I was taking photos of flowers when I got separated from my friends, and then I hurt my ankle."

"I'm sorry you were hurt, but I'm not sorry I found you."

She leaned forward and added a stick to the small fire he had kindled. "I promise, I was going to look for you as soon as we got back from the hike." She glanced at him. "You saved me a lot of trouble, walking right up to me like that."

"I never stopped looking for you," he said. "But I wasn't having much luck. The name thing threw me."

She winced. "I'm so—"

"No. I understand why you did it. But why Rosie Kenley?"

"My grandpa always called me Rosie, and Kenley was my mother's maiden name." She shrugged. "I didn't want to make things too complicated."

"It felt a little strange, thinking of you as Roslyn at first, but I like it. It suits you."

"Thanks." She would always have fond memories of him calling her Rosie, but better to put that behind her.

"Did you use your real name when you registered at the hotel?" he asked.

"I had to. That's the name on my ID and my credit card. But I told the desk clerks I was hiding from a stalker and to not tell anyone I was there. They were very sympathetic and helpful." She frowned. "It wasn't a lie, either. The press really had been stalking me for weeks at that point."

"You were a big celebrity in Chicago?"

"It was that slow a news period." She added another twig to the fire. "I think a lot of it was because the station had played up my romance with Matt so much. And I went right along with it. I was angry with Matt for being so ambitious and putting his career ahead of everything, but I was just as driven. I never objected to any of the ways he and the station manager suggested for us to promote ourselves. I believed it would benefit my career, too."

"It sounds like you really needed a getaway by the time you came to Brundage."

"It was Valentine's weekend, remember?" She smiled ruefully. "The radio station was doing a big promo for the holiday and everywhere I turned I saw another billboard or ad. I was determined to get far away until the holiday was over."

"I'm glad you did," he said. "It was one of the best Valentine's Days I've had."

Me, too, she thought, but she couldn't say it. Not yet. She had been too free with such declarations in the past and her words had come back to wound her.

"How did you get into being a DJ?" He added a large piece of wood to the fire. "It sounds like interesting work."

"It is. I love music and originally wanted to be on the production side, but there aren't a lot of jobs in that field, and it's still a very male-dominated profession. I started DJing when I was still in college and worked for several small stations around Chicago before I got a break at WZPR." Her voice trailed away. How to explain what had happened there without sounding self-pitying?

"You don't have to talk about it if you don't want to," he said.

"No. I want to tell you." She shifted, trying to get more comfortable. "It was like any new job at first," she said. "I started at the bottom—working in the middle of the night. But listeners liked me, and I gradually worked my way up to midmorning. I was aiming for morning drive time, but I wasn't allowed to carry a prime time slot on my own. Finally, I was paired with Mad Matt Judson!—always written with an exclamation point after his name in all the promos. He'd been working with another man for a couple of years, but that person moved on to a bigger market. I was excited about having a chance to show what I could do." She paused for a breath. "Later on, Matt told me he was upset that the station wouldn't let him be a solo act. I think we initially bonded over our frustration with station management."

"So the two of you hit it off right away?"

"We did. He was charming, or so I thought. He paid a lot of attention to me and flirted a lot—on and off the air. The listeners loved it, but I wasn't so sure. It was fun, but I didn't want to date him because I didn't think getting involved with a coworker would be okay. I kept turning him down when he asked me out, but one day the station manager pulled me aside and said the attraction between us was obvious and it was okay with the station if we pursued a relationship."

"That seems a little weird," Dillon said.

"In hindsight, it does. At the time, I was so naive I thought it meant they cared about me and wanted me to be happy. Matt and I started dating and I wanted to keep things quiet, but he insisted we didn't have anything to hide and made a point of telling everyone about us on-air. I was upset about that, but he said it was no big deal. The first of many warning signs I failed to heed."

Dillon balanced the pot of water on the fire. "Why did you split up?" he asked. "Or is that none of my business?"

She had told so few people about that time. It felt good to pour out the whole story to someone who cared, yet was objective. Dillon didn't know the people involved, except her. And she felt he wouldn't judge her, at least not as harshly as she had already judged herself. "We got engaged," she said. "Matt popped the question on-air. It was a very big deal. The station made a huge production of the whole thing. I was embarrassed, but also, well, who doesn't like to be made a fuss over? Part of me thought we were rushing things. It was too soon. But I felt backed into a corner. And after a while, I could see that our ratings were climbing. Management kept telling us this was great for our careers. And Matt wasn't the only one who was ambitious. I let my aspirations overrule any qualms I had." She sighed. "At first it was all good. Matt was attentive and romantic. But he refused to talk about a wedding or plans. He said we should milk the engagement hype—our ratings were skyrocketing." She smoothed her hands over the baby bump. "I tried to talk to him about having a family and he was adamant he didn't want children."

"So that was the beginning of the end."

"Not really." She sighed again. "I was still blissfully naive. And I thought I could change his mind about children. Then one day I overheard Matt talking to another DJ. The guy told him it looked like he might actually have to marry me. Matt told him that wasn't the plan—he was going to milk the engagement hype long enough to get picked up by a bigger market. Once that was done, it was bye-bye Roz."

"That must have been devastating." Dillon spoke softly, but the steel in his voice sent a shiver through her.

"I was a mess," she said. "I tried really hard to remain professional, but I was also so angry. Matt had proposed on-air, so I thought about breaking up with him on-air, too, but I knew that would be risking my job. So instead, I gave him back the ring when we were alone one evening. Then I went to management, told them we were no longer engaged and that I needed to be moved to another time slot. Matt could handle the morning slot by himself. I even said I was sure the listeners would love it."

"What did management say?" Dillon asked.

"They told me if I wouldn't work with Matt, I couldn't work for them. And just like that—I had no fiancé and no job. And then Matt went on-air the next morning and played the jilted lover card and everything blew up. I went from Chicago's darling to the most hated woman in town. People yelled terrible things at me from passing cars when I walked down the street. Photographers stalked me, newspapers and television covered the story. It was ridiculous. Looking back, I realize the station was probably feeding the frenzy in order to up ratings for Matt's show, but at the time I just felt like I was drowning and couldn't catch my breath."

"You should sue the station," Dillon said.

She nodded. "I thought about it, but in the end I just wanted to put the whole experience behind me. Coming to Brundage Mountain on vacation was the first step in making a fresh start. Meeting you— spending that weekend with you—I felt like I started healing then. You helped me more than you could know."

He put his arm around her and pulled her close. Just held her, his warmth encircling her, his strength pushing back some of the weariness and pain. "I understand better now why you didn't tell me the truth about who you were. Maybe in your position I would have done the same thing."

"When I met you, I really didn't want to be that person anymore," she said. "It was nice to be Rosie— a woman who attracted the attention of a fabulous, handsome man. Not Roslyn, who had screwed up everything."

"What happened wasn't your fault," he said.

"In some ways, it was. I ignored my own misgivings about the situation. I told myself I needed to go along with everything in order to make it in my chosen career." She let out a deep breath. "If nothing else, this whole experience has taught me to be more discerning."

"I'm glad you told me now," he said. "Though maybe it's just as well I didn't know about all of this back in February. I would have been tempted to follow you back to Chicago and teach a lesson to a certain DJ. Not to mention his bosses."

She laughed. "One look at you and I think they would have been shaking in their shoes." Dillon's dark good looks, not to mention muscular build, would be enough to make anyone think twice about arguing with him. And Matt had never impressed her as being particularly brave. He took the easiest path through life, including going along with a fake engagement in order to improve ratings.

Dillon opened both packets of food, then added hot water from the pot and sealed them again. "Five minutes to dinner," he said. "I'm going to feed Bentley, then I'll make chocolate."

He poured kibble he had stowed in his pack into Bentley's portable bowl and the dog crunched it down while Dillon made hot chocolate to accompany their meal.

Roslyn struggled not to wolf down the food. "It's not gourmet, but it's not bad," Dillon said.

"I'm so hungry I could eat almost anything," she said. "Though I'm glad I didn't have to."

"When we're done, I want to take a look at your ankle," he said.

"All right."

They finished the meal in silence, then he rinsed the cups and forks and returned them, along with the trash, to his pack. "Now let's see that ankle." He patted his leg, motioning for her to rest her ankle on his thigh.

She removed her boot and sock, then lifted her bound foot into his lap. He carefully unwound the bandage, his fingers warm and deft. "It's still pretty swollen," he said. "Does it hurt?"

"Not as much now that I've had a chance to rest it."

"The water in the creek is pretty cold. If you could hike down there, you could soak it."

"I'm too tired to go anywhere else tonight," she said.

He probed gently at her ankle, then began to massage her foot. She closed her eyes and bit back a moan. "I'll give you ten hours and twenty minutes to stop that," she said.

He slid his hands up to her calf and began gently kneading there. This time she did moan. "That feels amazing," she said.

"It feels pretty good from this side, too."

She opened her eyes and met his gaze, then he looked away and took his hands from her also. "I'll let you get some rest," he said. "We've got a long day ahead of us tomorrow."

Her body needed that rest, she knew. But her mind

insisted on thinking about all the other things they could be doing together, here alone in this cave, with only the soft glow of the firelight. His touch had awakened a lot of pleasant memories in her body. Memories she very much would like to repeat. She had told him she was smarter about relationships now, but was that really true? She was ready to jump back into Dillon's arms after five months apart when she still knew very little about him. Her instincts told her he was a good man, but those instincts had proved her wrong before.

DILLON LAY ON his back in the dark, the bed of pine boughs offering limited cushioning from the rock floor of the cave. He closed his eyes and told himself he needed to sleep, but he was too aware of Roslyn, only a few inches away from him in the dark. He imagined he could feel the heat of her body and smell the floral-and-vanilla scent of her perfume. The space blanket crackled with every shift of her body as she tried to get comfortable.

He'd gotten a little carried away, massaging her leg, the feel of her in his hands awakening memories of how wonderful it had felt to make love to her. She had been so responsive, and they had been so in sync with each other...

He had forced himself to move away from her. The last thing she needed right now was for him to come on too strong. She had made it clear what he had been to her—a weekend break from her troubled life back in Chicago. A way to jump-start her healing. She was willing for him to have a part in their child's life, though how much of a part she hadn't said, but she gave no indication she wanted anything else from him.

If she really had feelings for him—the kind of feelings he was beginning to have for her—she wouldn't have waited five months to contact him. For all he was ready to forgive her for concealing her true identity, he couldn't get over the fact that she had waited so long to let him know about the baby.

He rolled onto his side, blanket and branches crackling, and focused on his breathing. In on four counts. Hold four counts. Out four counts. Roslyn seemed to have settled down. He thought she might even be asleep.

Don't think about her, he reminded himself. *Don't think about anything*.

Breathe in four counts. Hold four counts. *What was that noise?* He held his breath, listening. Yes, a faint scraping noise. Like a footstep on the path outside the cave. Carefully, he pushed the blanket away and sat, wincing as it crackled beneath him. He waited long minutes and heard nothing.

Maybe he had imagined the sound. Or it was a small animal scurrying, or dried leaves stirring in the wind?

Then he heard it again, and adrenaline surged through him. Something was out there. Maybe just an animal.

He looked toward Roslyn. She lay on her side with her back to him, a dark silhouette in the fading firelight. Dillon rose, shoved his bare feet into his boots and tightened the laces. Bentley appeared at his side, watching him intently, ears forward, tail wagging slowly from side to side. Dillon patted the dog's side, then crept toward the cave opening. He moved outside, the dog at his side, intent on finding out if he was imagining a threat, or if they were really in danger.

Chapter Seven

Emma did not have time Friday evening to stop by the Jasper Police Department, but she was going to make time. Some things could be overlooked, but not this. She pushed her way through the television crews and spectators on the sidewalk outside the police station and into the front lobby. Department secretary Teresa Norwood moved to intercept her as she headed toward the doors leading to the heart of the station. "Emma, you look upset," Teresa said. Her warm, motherly manner betrayed a keen perceptiveness, but Emma supposed there wasn't anything subtle about her obvious anger.

"I need to speak to Captain Rutledge," Emma said. "And to the chief, if he's here."

"I've been telling the chief for the last hour that he needs to call it a day, but you know how stubborn he can be."

"As stubborn as you, since you're still here." The chief joined the two women. "What do you need, Emma?"

Emma glanced at Teresa, who had moved to her

desk and was pretending to sort papers, but was as alert as any retriever on the hunt. "Let's discuss this in your office," she said.

Walters escorted her to his office. Emma glanced into the office across from him and spotted Captain Rutledge. She leaned in to address him. "Lucy Green told me what happened at her place this afternoon," she said. "You scared her and her son half to death. You could have killed someone."

Rutledge rose from behind his desk. "That mutt of hers attacked me. I had every right to defend myself."

The chief moved past Emma into Rutledge's office. "Close the door, Emma, and let's discuss this," he said. Always the calm voice in a storm, she thought. They were all going to miss him when he retired.

"That dog—" Rutledge began, but Walters held up a hand to silence him. "Emma, you go first. What did Lucy Green tell you that has you so upset?"

"First of all, Captain Rutledge told her she couldn't take her dog with her when she evacuated this afternoon. That was a lie and completely uncalled for."

"The dog was racing around, barking like a maniac," Rutledge said. "It wouldn't come when Mrs. Green called and I didn't have all day to wait around. We'd had a report that the fire was near the exit road. If it jumped the ditch and crossed the road, we'd all be trapped. She needed to forget about the dog and leave."

"Peaches was upset, but instead of trying to calm

everyone down, the captain escalated the situation," Emma said. "Lucy came to me crying. I told her to file a formal complaint, but after what happened, she was too afraid."

"That dog attacked me," Rutledge said. "I had every right to defend myself."

She turned on him, all her fury unleashed. "That dog was a fifteen-pound, ten-year-old toy poodle. He doesn't even have most of his teeth. You were never in any danger." She turned back to Walters. "Lucy said Captain Rutledge drew his gun and threatened to shoot Peaches. Her seven-year-old son, Carter, rushed between Rutledge and the dog to protect it. If that gun had gone off, he could have been killed."

The lines on the chief's face were deeper than ever. "Arthur, is this true?"

Rutledge's face flushed crimson. "I was trying to help the woman with her dog, which wouldn't stop barking and refused to cooperate. I was going to pick it up and put it in her car for her and it tried to bite me."

"If an angry giant started yelling and grabbed you by the neck, you'd try to defend yourself, too," Emma said. "I know Lucy and I know her dog. I've worked with Peaches. He was a puppy mill dog and was abused. I'm sure he was terrified and defended himself the only way he knew how." She glared at Rutledge. "Pulling a gun was out of line."

"I want a full report on my desk by tomorrow morning," Walters said. When Rutledge started to protest, the chief added, "You drew your service weapon in a situation with civilians. That requires a full report. You know that. I could suspend you, effective immediately."

"I was defending myself. And the kid rushed in out of nowhere."

"I'm taking into consideration that you truly believe that, but don't let it happen again. And there will be a disciplinary review." He turned back to Emma. "Do you want to file a complaint?"

She stood up straighter, a little calmer now that she had gotten the story out in the open. "No. I want to offer Captain Rutledge a free training session at Daniels Canine Academy," she said. "I want him to learn how to properly interact with dogs."

"That's ridiculous," Rutledge protested. "A complete waste of my time."

"You're going to have plenty of free time if you don't watch yourself," Walters said. "What exactly are you talking about, Emma?"

"I've been thinking for some time that it would be a good idea for first responders to have training on how to interact safely with dogs. At many of the calls they respond to, they're confronted with family pets who may be upset and protective. Dogs are very sensitive and they pick up on the tension around them. Knowing how to de-escalate that tension in the dogs as well as the people could make it easier for police, firefighters and EMTs to do their jobs and could prevent injury to both animals and people." She turned to Rutledge. "You can be my first student, and help me iron out any wrinkles in the program."

"I don't—" Rutledge began.

But Walters interrupted him. "What Emma is describing sounds like an excellent program. It wouldn't be a bad idea for all our officers to go through similar training. You can be the first."

"I can't possibly take time out from my duties for that now," Rutledge said. "Not with this fire, and a killer to track down."

"You can schedule the class later," the chief said. "But I'm making it a requirement."

Rutledge wanted to argue, she could see, but he clamped his mouth shut. She and the chief moved out of his office, back toward the lobby. "Thank you," she said. "And I'm sorry I stormed in here so upset."

"I think your anger was justified, and I think the course you're designing is a good way to address the problem. So thank you."

She started to say goodbye but hung back. Something else Rutledge had said was nagging at her. "What's this about a killer?" she asked.

"You haven't seen the story on the news?"

"I haven't had time to listen to the news. I've had my hands more than full with my own dogs and the evacuees' pets, not to mention the press."

"The press have been bothering you?"

"They're looking for human-interest stories related to the wildfire. I understand, and I know the publicity could be good for DCA, but I don't have the bandwidth to deal with them right now. Brady helped escort the last bunch off the property this afternoon."

"Don't hesitate to call if they show up again. I'll send an officer to clear them out."

"Thanks. I hope I don't need that. But what about this killer?"

"I don't think he's anything for you to worry about. The Idaho State University killer, Kent Anderson, escaped the South Boise Prison complex a couple of days ago and is supposedly headed here. We haven't had a definite sighting since a tourist claimed to have dropped him off on the north side of town. But keep an eye out for anyone suspicious hanging around."

"One thing about having dozens of dogs on the premises," she said. "No one sneaks up on us." Another worry intruded. "Any word about Dillon? Someone told me he and Bentley went out to search for a lost hiker and were cut off by the fire."

"Nothing to report there, though they would have had to get pretty far off track to be in an active burn area. We think they're having to take a circuitous route back to town and are out of phone range."

"I hope they're okay." She had a soft spot for the handsome cop, not to mention his dog.

"Anything else I can do for you?" Walters asked.

"Just keep Captain Rutledge away from dogs."

AT HOME FRIDAY EVENING, Ava changed into leggings and a sweatshirt and switched on the TV while she puttered around the house. Lacey had made herself comfortable on the sofa. Eli was working late tonight, so Ava heated leftovers for dinner and settled on the sofa beside the dog. "You can't take up all the room," she said as she scooted Lacey over to make a place for herself.

"Two searches with very different aims continue tonight outside Jasper, Idaho, as authorities hunt for escaped mass murderer Kent Anderson, who is reported to be at large in the area of the Gem Creek fire. The wildfire has consumed over twelve thousand acres of public land in the area, but threatens several neighborhoods. Also missing in the vicinity is former Chicago DJ Roz Kern, who disappeared while hiking with friends shortly before the trail she was on was closed by authorities due to the fire danger."

Ava leaned forward and punched the remote to up the volume on the television as a sandy-haired woman with large glasses appeared on the left half of the split screen. White block letters beneath her identified her as "Rockin' Roz's Best Friend." "With us this evening we have Cheri Benton," the female news anchor, a Latinx woman with short dark hair and large gold hoop earrings, said. "Cheri, you were hiking with Roz this morning, is that correct?"

"Um, yes, that's right."

"And how did Roz seem to you this morning?" the anchor asked.

"She likes to be called Roslyn now." Cheri tucked a strand of hair behind one ear and shifted in her chair. "She was fine. Looking at the scenery and taking pictures and stuff."

The anchor's image was replaced by a picture of a slight woman with shoulder-length blond hair and a harried expression. Obviously a candid shot taken on a city street, this was a far cry from the glamorous woman in the publicity shot that the police department had received when Roslyn first disappeared.

"Roz—Roslyn—Kern was a top-rated disc jockey for Chicago rock station WZPR until January of this year, when she abruptly broke her engagement with morning drive-time partner, Matthew 'Mad Matt' Judson, and left the radio station. Since this, Ms. Kern has avoided the public eye and refused to answer questions about her erratic behavior."

"Maybe she didn't think she owed anyone an explanation for her private decision," Ava said.

The anchor's image replaced the photo of Roslyn. "Cheri, I understand your friend is pregnant."

"Yes." Cheri looked uncomfortable.

"Who is the baby's father?" the anchor—Ava thought her name was Val—asked.

"I don't know," Cheri said. "Roslyn never said and I respected her privacy."

"We spoke with Matt Judson and he denies being the father of Roz's child."

"Oh, Matt definitely isn't the father," Cheri said. "I know that much."

"Why did Roz come to Idaho?" Val asked. "Does she know someone here?"

"No. She just came on vacation. Like we did. We ran into each other in the coffee shop in Jasper this morning and all decided to go hiking together." Cheri's voice broke. "I should have stayed with her when she told me to go ahead. I could have waited while she took her pictures and we could have walked back together. If I'd done that, she would be here now."

"Perhaps Roz wanted you to leave her," Val said. "Maybe she came to Idaho intending to disappear."

Cheri shook her head, eyes wide. "No. She wouldn't do that."

"Does Roz know Kent Anderson?" Val asked.

Cheri frowned. "Who is that?"

Another photo appeared on the screen, this one a mug shot of a man with thinning brown hair, a sharp nose and a grim expression. "In May of last year, Kent Anderson, a former teaching assistant at Idaho State University, entered a classroom carrying a semiautomatic rifle and shot and killed six people, including a professor. He was sentenced to life in prison last month and was awaiting transfer to the supermax facility in Florence, Colorado, when he escaped and headed straight for Jasper, Idaho, where he vanished in the same location where Roslyn Kern disappeared."

"Roslyn didn't know him," Cheri protested. "How could she?"

"Thank you for talking with us, Cheri," Val said. Cheri's image disappeared and the shot widened to show Val and a U-shaped desk with a handsome older man with swept-back silvering hair.

"That's quite a coincidence," the man said. "Two

people disappearing on the same day in the same remote area."

"Roz Kern and Kent Anderson are about the same age," Val said. "His trial was just beginning when she dumped her fiancé and left her job at the radio station."

"Why would a young woman with a stellar career and a devoted fiancé leave everything and disappear into obscurity, only to turn up pregnant a few months later, refusing to talk about the father of her unborn child, then abruptly head to Idaho and drop off the map?" The male anchor shook his head, his expression somewhere between concern and scolding. "It's a mystery you can be sure we'll be following closely."

Ava switched off the television. Considering Kent Anderson had been under lock and key for the better part of the last two years, the idea that he might be the father of the baby being carried by a young woman in Chicago was ludicrous. But plenty of people would latch on to the idea. Heaven help Roslyn Kern when she did surface again.

She picked at her meal but finally gave up and hugged a pillow to her chest. Everything about the news report had unsettled her, from the nervous, on-the-spot friend, to the snide innuendo of the anchors. Maybe it was because she and Roslyn Kern were close to the same age, and she had been a single woman on her own in Chicago.

She leaned over and hugged Lacey. "Dillon and Bentley will find Roslyn Kern," she said. "But I'd just as soon Kent Anderson stayed far away."

A QUICK RECONNAISSANCE of the path on either side of the cave showed no one and nothing disturbed that Dillon could see. Bentley sniffed the ground and whined, a faint, low sound that Dillon took to be a question as to why they were even out here at this time of night, instead of sleeping. He stood for a moment outside the cave, breathing in the air that still carried a faint hint of smoke, the utter silence of the moment surrounding him. Some of the tension eased from his shoulders. The noise he had heard was probably only a pack rat, or the wind. Finding Roslyn again, learning about the baby, detouring because of the fire—the tensions of the day were getting to him. Time to relax and get some sleep.

He turned to walk back toward the cave as a woman's scream cut through the air, stopping his heart, then sending him running.

Bentley was faster, barking furiously at the figure that emerged from the cave, running in the opposite direction. Man and dog gave chase, Bentley sounding the alarm and speeding forward. The figure left the path, crashing through the brush as it leaped toward the creek, like an elk bounding through the forest. But this was no elk. "Stop! Police!" Dillon called, but the fleeing man kept going. Dillon ran until his sides ached. Bentley had stopped barking, and though the thick underbrush slowed him, he kept powering through, until Dillon called him back. "Bentley, come!" he commanded, and the dog obediently wheeled around and headed back to him.

He stared into the darkness, though he could no

longer see whoever he had been pursuing. This must have been the person Bentley had alerted them about earlier today. Who was he and what was he doing, following them?

He bent over, trying to catch his breath, waiting for Bentley to reach him, then he remembered the scream. Roslyn! He turned and pounded back down the trail. "Roslyn!" he called as he neared the cave. "Roslyn, are you all right?"

"I'm fine." Her voice was strong and steady. She met him at the entrance to the cave. "Who was that?" she asked. "I woke up and someone was right by me. At first I thought it was you, then I realized it wasn't. That's when I screamed."

He shook his head and ushered her back inside. He sat beside the fire and stirred the coals, and began feeding in small pieces of tinder to get the blaze going again. He wanted the light and heat the fire would give. She settled onto the log beside him. "Was someone really there?"

"Someone was there," he said. "Bentley and I chased after him, but he got away."

She hugged herself. "Do you think it was the same person Bentley sensed was following us on the trail?"

"I don't know. You go on back to sleep. I'm going to stay up in case whoever it was comes back."

"No way could I sleep now," she said. "Let's have some tea." She turned and reached back for the packs they had piled behind the logs, then froze. "Dillon? Where's my pack?"

"It's not with mine?" He turned to look.

"No." She looked around. "Do you think whoever was here took it?"

He slipped a flashlight from his pack and shone it around the cave. They found the pack on the floor near the cave entrance, the contents spilling from it. Roslyn's camera bag was a few feet closer to the entrance. She picked up the bag and opened it. "The camera is still here," she said.

"He was probably trying to steal the pack when your scream startled him," Dillon said.

"The whole pack, or just the camera?" She removed the camera from the pack and switched it on. "It doesn't seem damaged."

Dillon came to stand beside her. "Why would a thief want your camera? Especially here in the middle of nowhere?"

She shook her head. "It's worth some money but not out here." She started to switch it off, but he covered her hand with his, stopping her. "What did you photograph today?" he asked.

"Wildflowers. Some shots of the fire and scenery."

"Let me see."

She handed him the camera and showed him how to scroll through the photos. He scanned close-ups of brilliantly colored wildflowers and wider shots of the scenery, smoke clouds making for dramatic skies as a backdrop to mountain peaks and wildflower-filled meadows. He stopped on a photo that showed rocks in the distance, and a figure standing against the rocks. "Who is this?" he asked.

She leaned over his shoulder to look. "I don't know," she said. "I was focused on that patch of paintbrush and sunflowers, not the background."

"Could it be one of the friends you were hiking with?"

She took the camera from him, pressed a few buttons, then studied the screen again. She had enlarged the photo and zoomed in on the figure in the background. The image wasn't clear, but it was clearly a man with very short dark hair and pale skin, dressed in a black T-shirt and khaki trousers. "It's not anyone I know," she said. She looked up, her green eyes troubled. "Do you think it's the person who's been following us?"

"Maybe." He studied the photograph for a long moment, then switched off the camera. "Maybe he knew you took that photo of him and he doesn't like the idea. He followed us and waited until he thought we were asleep, then tried to steal the camera."

"The idea gives me the creeps." She replaced the camera in its case, and stuffed it into her pack and returned the pack to rest next to Dillon's.

"I should have kept after him," Dillon said. "Maybe Bentley and I could have caught up with him."

She slipped her arm into his and leaned close. "I'm glad you didn't leave me here by myself," she said. "I feel safer with you around." She stretched up and kissed him, a gentle pressure from her lips, her arms moving around him, urging him closer.

His earlier restraint fell away in the warmth of

that kiss. If she wanted this, then he definitely wasn't going to argue. "I've missed you," she murmured as her lips traced a trail down his throat.

"I missed you, too." He shaped his hand to her breast, reveling in the new fullness.

She arched against him, the baby bump pressing into his stomach, the sensation new, but somehow thrilling. "Maybe now isn't the best time or place," she said. "But I really want to make love with you."

"Yeah. I want that, too." It was crazy—they hadn't seen each other in five months, and he had spent so much of that time angry and confused over his feelings about her. But now that they were here all he could feel was how much he wanted her. Not Rosie Kenley, but Roslyn Kern. The beautiful, bewitching woman who was going to have his baby.

He stood and pulled her to her feet beside him, then traced his hands down her sides and over the hard round curve of her abdomen. "Sexy, huh?" she teased.

"Yes." He crushed his lips to hers, letting her know just how sexy he found her. They moved together, kissing and caressing, a dance without music, until finally she led him to the bed of pine boughs. Before they lay down, he reached down and flicked away the space blanket. "I draw the line at making love on a bed of aluminum foil," he said.

She laughed, the sound sending a new rush of heat through him. "I agree, but I don't really want pine needles poking me in the back."

"Wait just a minute." He returned to their packs

and pulled out the extra jackets they both carried. He spread these over the pine needles, then eased down and pulled her on top of him. Not bad. And when she straddled him and began kissing him again, it wouldn't have mattered if he had lain directly on the ground. All he felt was her against him, stirring a need that had never really abated since they had parted five months ago.

She started undressing and he lay back, wishing the light was better, though on second thought, the play of flickering firelight across her breasts, her bare shoulders and her face was an erotic show he didn't think he would ever tire of watching. Her breasts were fuller now, her body more rounded and sensual. When she was naked, she knelt beside him, the sexiest sight he had ever seen. "Now it's your turn," she said and reached to unbutton his jeans.

Chapter Eight

Roslyn remembered what Dillon had been like in bed before—so confident, sure of himself, clearly practiced in pleasing a woman. He enjoyed sex and made sure she enjoyed it, too. They had had fun together, something she had needed so badly just then.

The man who was stripping off his clothing in front of her now was the same, and different, too. Being with him now felt more intense. Urgent. They had a history together now. They had made the child she carried inside her, and that added to the moment an excitement she hadn't known before.

He lay back on their makeshift bed and beckoned her. "I think it will be more comfortable for you on top," he said. His gaze swept over her body and a grin spread across his face. "And I get to enjoy such a great view."

She had been self-conscious about undressing in front of him, but had made herself get it over with, telling herself he wouldn't see that much in the firelight. But what he saw obviously pleased him, and the desire in his eyes made her own need for him more urgent.

She straddled him, his erection hot at her entrance, but she made him wait, moving in a sensuous dance against him, tracing her fingers over his chest and stomach, rubbing against him until they were both panting with need. His fingers grasped her hips. "You're driving me wild," he said. Then he slid one hand around to touch her and she moaned.

Hands flat on his chest, she pushed herself up and slid over him, the sensation of him filling her stealing her breath for a moment. She had missed this so much. She had missed him.

With his hands, he coaxed her to move, and with his mouth he caressed her face and then her breasts. She trembled with her need for him and tried to hold back, to make the moment last, but he wouldn't let her. He knew just how to touch her to bring her to completion and she didn't have the will to resist. She didn't want to resist, and before long her climax shuddered through her, with an intensity she didn't remember from before.

He grew still, holding her, and she stared down at him, dazed and unable to stop smiling. Then he began to move again, and her with him. She stroked the side of his face and his chest, and moved with care to give him pleasure. She was rewarded when he cried out and arched upward. She rode the wave of his climax, then collapsed onto him, his arms tight around her, her body cradled between his legs.

It was a long time before either of them spoke.

She slid off him and lay by his side, her head in the hollow of his shoulder, his arm still around her. "We should probably check if the packs are still here," she said after a while. "I think anyone could have come in while we were busy and I wouldn't have noticed."

"Bentley would have let us know," Dillon said.

At the sound of his name the dog, who lay by the fire with his back to them, as if to give them privacy, raised his head and gave a single thump of his tail. "Good boy," Dillon said, and Bentley lay down again, silent.

"I wish I knew who the man was in that picture," she said.

But Dillon didn't answer. He breathed deeply and evenly beside her, already asleep.

Trapped By Wildfire
Rockin' Roz Risks All on Wilderness Hike

Former Chicago DJ Roslyn "Rockin' Roz" Kern took what began as an innocent hike while on vacation in Jasper, Idaho, last Friday. But the pleasant outing with friends turned into a dangerous one as Roz ended up lost in the wilderness, her path back to civilization cut off by an out-of-control wildfire.

Many residents of the Windy City know Roz from her top-rated morning drive-time show with fellow DJ—and former fiancé—Matthew "Mad Matt" Judson. Roz abruptly left the station in January, following a breakup with Mad

Matt that had the airwaves buzzing. Though she has kept a low profile since then, this paper recently learned that Roz is expecting a baby. Is the father Mad Matt? And was Roz's hike really so innocent? Despairing about her broken engagement and future as an unemployed single mom, did Roz deliberately leave her friends, searching for another way to end her dilemma?

Authorities in Jasper are supposedly searching for Roz, but the wildfire is hampering their efforts. Several neighborhoods in the area have been evacuated and local residents are worried about their safety as the fire nears the small town.

"THIS SO-CALLED REPORTER must be making things up as he goes along." Brady tossed aside the printout from a website that Teresa had handed out to the gathered officers. "She talks like the fire is racing toward town unchecked. Jasper isn't in any danger, and those neighborhoods were evacuated as a precaution, not because anyone was in immediate danger."

"This one is worse." Ava passed over another printout, this one from a Chicago tabloid. "Rockin' Roz pursued by deadly killer while fleeing wilderness fire," she read. She tossed the paper aside. "I saw a television story last night where the anchors tried to insinuate that Roslyn Kern came here and ditched her friends so she could meet up with Kent Anderson. They even tried to insinuate that Anderson might be the father of Kern's unborn child. Never mind that he's been in jail for two years."

"Stranger things have happened," Brady said.

"Oh, please," Ava said. "We have no idea where Roslyn Kern or Kent Anderson are, but there's no reason to believe they're close to each other."

"What about Roslyn being pregnant?" Jason asked. "Did Dillon say anything about that in his message to you?"

Brady shook his head. "All the text says is that he found Roslyn and they planned to spend the night in those caves above Cow Creek and head back on the trail today." He leaned back in his chair. "I sent a reply asking if he needed anything, or wanted someone to hike out to meet them, but I never heard back."

"From what I remember, cell reception is terrible there around the creek," Ava said.

The door opened and the chief entered and everyone sat up straighter. Even Lacey, Ava's police K-9, grew more alert, focused on the podium at the front of the room. The bags under Chief Walters's eyes were fuller, the lines around his mouth and across his forehead deeper. Brady suspected he had worked late and come in early. Behind him, Captain Rutledge looked fresh and crisp, a commander straight out of Central Casting, except he didn't have the character to go with the image.

After a brief pause, two more men entered. Captain Eli Thorne from the McCall, Idaho, police department was familiar to them from a case they had worked recently, involving a disgruntled employee setting bombs around town. He and Ava had become involved during that investigation and seemed pretty serious about each other now. But what was he doing here this morning?

Behind Eli was a fifty-something man with the lean build of a runner and close-cropped salt-and-pepper hair. He wore a suit, but everything about him, from his erect posture to the hard look in his eyes as he scanned the room, screamed law enforcement. "Looks like a Fed," Ava whispered next to him.

"Brady, do you have any more messages from Dillon?" the chief asked.

"No, sir," Brady said.

"Anyone else heard from Dillon?" Walters asked.

Everyone shook their heads.

Walters looked down at the papers in front of him. "As you can see from the articles and online postings Teresa printed for us, there's a lot of interest from the press in this Roslyn Kern. Apparently, she's something of a celebrity in Chicago."

"A pregnant celebrity lost in an out-of-control wildfire, pursued by a dangerous killer," Ava said, her voice carrying plenty of snark.

Walters's scowl showed what he thought of that assessment. "I spoke with the incident commander this morning and he estimates the Gem Creek fire is thirty-five percent contained. There's still activity near Skyline Road, so we're going to keep that area closed for another day. The slurry bomber will be working in there this morning. Spotters overnight pinpointed areas hotshot crews will focus on."

"Did the spotters see any sign of Dillon and Roslyn Kern?" Cal Hoover asked.

"Not of them," Walters said.

"If they were in the caves by Cow Creek, they wouldn't have been visible from the air," Brady said.

"You said 'not of them,'" Lieutenant Margaret Avery said. A veteran of Jasper PD, Margaret had a reputation as an excellent detective. "Did the spotters see someone else?"

Walters plucked a sheet of paper from the pile in front of him. "A spotter plane flying over Williams Park saw a campfire, with a single camper visible, at approximately eleven fourteen p.m."

"How can he be sure it was a campfire, and not a remnant of the wildfire?" Rutledge asked.

"Apparently, they use infrared cameras that allow them to differentiate the heat generated by humans and animals from that of the fire," Walters said. "They were sure this was a person by a campfire."

"No one has reported any campers missing, and there are no cars at the trailhead," Jason said.

"I doubt that's a camper," Rutledge said. "We know Kent Anderson was last seen not far from the Williams Gap Trailhead."

"But what would he be doing way out there?" Ava asked.

"Deputy Rand from the US Marshals is here to address that."

Deputy Rand moved to the microphone. "The

US Marshals Service is in charge of the pursuit and apprehension of Kent Anderson. Following his escape from custody outside Kuna, Idaho, which resulted in the death of two law enforcement officers, we have tracked him to McCall, Idaho." He glanced over his shoulder. "Captain Thorne has more information about that."

Eli took Rand's place at the microphone. "We've received new information about Kent Anderson I wanted to share with you," he said. "We've tracked down his connection to this area—a woman named Deena Marquette. She's Anderson's cousin and they apparently grew up together. She and her boyfriend, Sean Tyson, moved to Jasper eight months ago. She and Anderson exchanged letters while he was in prison and apparently used a childhood code to pass messages that looked innocuous on the surface, but are now believed to have included plans for Anderson's escape. Prison authorities reviewed all of his correspondence after the escape and they think they've figured out the code. Marquette and Tyson agreed to place a cache of supplies for Anderson near the Williams Gap Trail—a backpack, food and water, and other equipment he could use to travel cross-country. Apparently, he planned to travel through backcountry all the way to Alaska."

"That could take months," Rutledge said.

"Anderson was willing to take the time," Thorne said. "Though Marquette and Tyson aren't admitting any part in the plan, she did say Anderson had a lot of experience camping and backpacking and liked being out of doors. He probably thought the fire would make good cover for his getaway."

"Do you think he's the lone camper the spotter saw?" Ava asked.

Eli started to answer, but Rand interrupted. "We don't think the camper spotted in the fire zone is Kent Anderson," he said. He nodded to Eli, a clear dismissal, and Eli yielded the podium. "We also interviewed Marquette and Tyson, as well as a friend of Anderson's, a man named Donald Aldeen, who lives in Yellow Pine, Idaho, and is purported to have been friends with Anderson since the third grade. He was very cooperative and says Anderson's plan is to head west to Nevada. We believe Marquette and Tyson made up the story about Alaska to deliberately mislead us. I'm here today to thank you all for your assistance with the search so far, but we'll be moving the pursuit to the west as of this morning."

"Have there been other reliable sightings of Anderson in the west?" Ava asked. Leave it to Ava to question the Feds while everyone else remained silent.

"We are not releasing any further information at this time," Rand said. "All you need to know is you don't have anything to worry about."

"What about all these stories in the news?" Captain Rutledge asked. "The media is needlessly frightening people by focusing on Anderson's supposed presence here."

"We don't have time to waste contradicting the media," Rand said. "Besides, it's to our benefit to have Anderson believe the search is still focused here." He stepped back and Walters moved to the microphone again.

"Thank you, Deputy Rand," he said. "I know you're very busy with this search, so we won't keep you any longer."

"Thank you, Chief." Rand nodded to the other man at the front of the room, then left.

Everyone waited a long beat until they were sure Rand was gone. "If that camper the spotters saw in the fire area isn't Anderson, who is it?" Lieutenant Cal Hoover asked. Tall and taciturn, Cal was an experienced officer and others listened when he spoke.

"It could be Dillon and Ms. Kern," Rutledge said.

"I have the coordinates where the camper was spotted," Walters said. He turned to the map behind him, consulted the paper in his hand, then positioned a red pin. "About here. About twenty yards off the Williams Gap trail, on the edge of that big open area known as Williams Park."

"Less than a mile from the Cow Creek caves," Brady said.

"We don't know for sure Dillon and Roslyn made it all the way to Cow Creek," Rutledge said. "The campfire could have been theirs."

"The report from the spotter says their equipment only picked up one person," Walters said.

"Do you know what other information the marshals have that makes them so sure Anderson isn't here?" Margaret asked.

"They seem to put a lot of stock in the information

they gleaned from Anderson's friend," Brady said. "Do we know anything about him? How likely is it that he's telling the truth?"

"You heard Deputy Rand," Rutledge said. "This isn't our concern."

"Except if they're wrong and that is Anderson out there, and Dillon is close to him, it is our concern," Ava said.

They all looked to the chief, waiting for his answer. "We have an unknown person in an area that is closed to the public," Walters said. "It makes sense to keep an eye on the situation and learn what we can about this person, as our schedule allows. But we have plenty of real crime to keep us busy here."

Chairs creaked as bodies shifted. "If the Feds are wrong and that is Anderson, does he know Dillon and Roslyn are on the same trail?" Brady asked.

"If he does, wouldn't he be moving away from them?" Jason asked.

"Most likely, yes," Thorne said. "Unless he's learned that Dillon is a law enforcement officer. He's made several public declarations, at his trial and in interviews he has given since his conviction, that he intends to kill any law enforcement officers who cross his path. He's attacked several officers in his time in prison, resulting in him spending much of his sentence in administrative segregation."

Solitary confinement, Brady translated. "How did he ever escape?" he asked.

"Ahead of his transfer to the federal supermax prison in Florence, Colorado," Thorne said. "An accomplice, one of the prison trustees, secreted a weapon in the transport van and Anderson used it to kill both his guards. He unlocked his restraints, stole some clothing, and hitchhiked to Jasper."

"He wouldn't know Dillon was an officer," Cal said. "He was on that trail as a search and rescue volunteer."

"The spotters are doing regular flyovers of the fire and we've asked them to keep an eye out for anyone," Walters said.

"Why not set a helicopter down in the area and send a team after this mysterious camper?" Rutledge asked. "If it does turn out to be Anderson, we'd be heroes."

"We don't have the budget to send a helicopter after someone who might not even be a threat," Walters said. "Thought I doubt we'd find a pilot who would agree to go in there. The terrain is very rough in that area, and visibility is poor because of the smoke, and most of the available aircraft are helping to fight the fire."

"If this is Anderson, depending on his position, he might spot a group of officers headed toward him," Eli said. "The letters he exchanged with his cousin indicate they agreed to supply him with guns and ammunition, and he had sworn to kill cops on sight."

"In any case, that decision is out of our hands," Walters said. "We can do some low-key investigating to try to learn the identity of the lone camper, but federal marshals are in charge of the pursuit of Anderson. Local forces are on call to assist."

"Someone should warn Dillon," Ava said. "A couple of us could hike up the trail to meet him."

"I've spoken to Search and Rescue about doing just that," Walters said. "I would send a couple of officers with them. But Commander Wayne says they're stretched to the max dealing with the usual demands of a holiday weekend. They've had three calls in the last two days, in addition to the search for Roslyn Kern. Another lost hiker, an ATV accident, and a white water rafting accident. Andrea pointed out that Dillon is an experienced rescue volunteer who is well equipped to spend a night out and he hasn't indicated he and Ms. Kern are in any kind of trouble."

"Roslyn Kern is pregnant," Jason said.

"That is a concern," Walters said. "I asked about getting a rescue helicopter to her — provided we could locate her and Dillon. But all air resources in the area are focused on fighting the wildfire. We'll keep trying to reach out to Dillon and searching for Anderson. In all probability, the marshals are right and Anderson is on his way to Nevada. Dillon and Ms. Kern are on their way back to Jasper, and Anderson is moving away from town as quickly as he can." He turned to Rutledge. "Captain, what do we have on the docket for today?"

Rutledge stepped forward and began reading off a list of the usual problems that accompanied a busy holiday weekend—illegal fireworks, minor traffic accidents, shoplifting, noise complaints and angry exchanges fueled by overindulgence in alcohol. "We also have the media harassing everyone in town," Rutledge concluded.

"The press is allowed to be here as long as they don't trespass on private property," Walters said.

"They are," Rutledge agreed. "But I think it would help calm the situation, and possibly quell some of the rumors that are spreading around, if we held a press conference to talk about the search for Anderson and for Dillon and Roz Kern."

"No," Walters said. "I don't have time to deal with the press."

"I could speak to them," Rutledge said. He smoothed back his hair. "I'm used to dealing with the media."

"No," Walters repeated. He scanned the room, his gaze sharp. "Any questions?" No one spoke up.

"Dismissed. Do a good job today."

Chairs scraped back and voices rose as everyone collected their belongings and filed out of the room. Thorne met Ava and Brady at the door. The McCall police captain had an imposing presence, but his stern face relaxed into a smile as Lacey leaned against him, tail wagging. "Sorry I can't stay longer," he told Ava as he rubbed the dog's ears. "McCall is even more crowded with visitors this weekend than Jasper. I'll call you later."

"Let us know if you hear anything more about Anderson," Ava said. "If I wasn't on duty today, I'd take Lacey for a hike out that way, just to have a look around."

"The trailhead is closed to the public," Brady said.

"Lacey and I aren't public," she said. "We're sworn law enforcement officers."

"Woof," Lacey barked, as if in agreement.

"One more reason for you both to stay far away from anyone who might be Anderson." Thorne kissed her cheek. "I'll see you later."

"See you." Ava watched him go, then turned to Brady. "Have you tried texting Dillon again? He needs to know about the other person who's out there near him. Even if it isn't Anderson, the person might be up to no good."

"I've tried calling and texting, but I'm not getting through."

She sighed. "At least he has Bentley with him."

"Bentley isn't a police dog—he's a search dog, like Winnie," Brady said. His dog, Winnie, a yellow Lab, was terrific at finding people, but her biggest asset was her friendly, gentle demeanor. "Search dogs aren't supposed to be threatening." Lacey didn't look particularly threatening at the moment, either, but the German shepherd was trained to take down criminals.

"Any dog would smell or hear someone approaching a long time before Dillon would know they were there," Ava said. "He can warn Dillon if they're being followed."

"I figure Dillon will need all the help he can get," Brady said. "He probably has his hands full with this Roslyn Kern—celebrity DJ who couldn't find her way on a marked hiking trail."

"You don't know what happened out there," Ava

said. "It's easy to get turned around if you're not familiar with the area, and with the fire and everything, anyone could get lost."

"You're right," Brady admitted. "I'm just worried about Dillon. I'll feel better when he's back home."

"We all will." She looked down at Lacey. "Come on, girl. Let's go distract the reporters." She grinned at Brady. "The cameras always zero in on Lacey."

"Jasper's finest," he said. He waited until they were gone and pulled out his phone and sent yet another text to Dillon. There's someone else out there with you—lone man. Could be escaped fugitive Kent Anderson or someone else, he wrote. Watch your six.

Chapter Nine

Dillon woke as soon as Roslyn got out of their make-shift bed. It wasn't noise that woke him, but the absence of her weight and warmth beside him. He opened his eyes to thin, gray light. "Is everything okay?" he asked.

"I'm fine." She retrieved her clothing from the cave floor and began to dress. "I just need to, um, use the bushes."

"Don't go too far." He told himself he should look away as she raised her arms to slide her tunic over her head or bent to pull on her jeans, but her body fascinated him—the lusher curves, and the swelling abdomen. Their baby. He tore his gaze away and found her watching him.

"I look a lot different now, I know," she said.

"You're beautiful." He sat up and reached for her. "If we were somewhere besides a cave in the middle of nowhere, I'd take you back to bed right now."

Heat flashed in her eyes. "I'll take a rain check on that offer." Her trained contralto voice made even an offhand comment like this sound sexy. She tugged her hand away from his. "Now, I really do have to go."

She finished dressing and slipped from the cave. He thought of the man he had chased away last night and rose to follow her to the entrance to the cave, where he stood and kept watch. But he saw no one, and heard nothing but birds beginning their morning chorus.

When he heard her returning, he moved to the fire ring and began coaxing a blaze from last night's coals. "Do you have more coffee?" she asked.

"Yes." He filled the pot with water and set it to heat.

She sank onto a log across from him. "I don't drink much caffeine these days but I really need a cup this morning." She rubbed at her ankle.

"Is the ankle bothering you?" he asked.

"Not much," she said, but her frown told him she was probably lying.

"Let me see." He moved over beside her and she shifted to allow him to remove her boot and sock. He probed at the puffy flesh around her anklebone. "I don't think it's as swollen as yesterday," he said.

"How many miles do we have to hike today?" she asked.

"About six." A long way over sometimes rough terrain on a painful ankle. "We'll take it slow."

She laughed. "I'm glad to hear it, since that's the only speed I'm capable of right now."

"How's the baby?" he asked.

She shaped both hands to the bump. "He, or she, is awake and raring to go."

He started to touch her, then hesitated. "Can I?" he asked.

"Of course." She smiled, the knowing grin of someone sharing a wonderful secret.

He placed his hand over the bump, fingers spread, and felt the flutter of movement beneath. That tiny sensation made him feel momentarily weightless.

"I know," she said, apparently interpreting the look on his face. "I'm still in awe."

His hand still on her, he met her gaze. "How did you feel when you found out?" he asked. "You can tell me the truth. This changed your whole life."

"I was shocked," she said. "And a little afraid. Raising a child—another human being—is such a big responsibility. And to do it alone..."

"You won't be alone," he said. Would she think he was presuming too much? "I want to be a part of my child's life," he added. Though he was beginning to hope he could be a part of her life, too.

"I want that, too," she said. "But when I first found out, I didn't know how you would feel. Some men feel blindsided by something like this. Resentful." She looked away. "It was one of the things Matt and I argued about, even before I found out our engagement was just a stunt to grab ratings."

He was beginning to really despise Mad Matt. "What do you mean?" he asked.

"He and I were talking, the way you do. I asked

him how many children he thought we should have. He said none. He was very firm about it, too. No kids. He said it was a deal breaker for him. I was shocked. I told myself that he loved me and he would change his mind, but looking back on it now, I think we would have split up over that even if I hadn't learned what was really going on." She smoothed her shirt over her belly. "Maybe he even told me that so he would have a good excuse to break things off when the time came."

"Does that mean you're okay with having a baby now?"

"I'm more than okay. I'm excited and happy." Her smile was genuine. Radiant. "Once the shock wore off and the reality set in, I realized that I was in as good a place as I could be to add a child to my life. I had a new career with a flexible schedule. I didn't have to answer to anyone but myself."

And now he was in the picture. Did she see that as a good thing—a partner to help raise this child—or as someone who would interfere? They had so many things to figure out, and only a few months to do so.

She bent forward and began pulling on her sock once more. "Don't worry about me today," she said. "I can be pretty stubborn when I set my mind to do something."

So could he, though he didn't say so. She would learn soon enough that he had made up his mind to look after her and the baby. After so many months of searching, he wasn't going to let her go again.

VALENTINE'S DAY AT Brundage Mountain Resort had
attracted a crowd. When Dillon had set out for the
resort that morning, he hadn't even thought about the
date, but it didn't take long to notice the heart deco-
rations everywhere, and the abundance of couples in
the lift lines, sliding forward two by two.

Which was one reason the woman in the black ski
pants and silver puffy jacket stood out in the crowd.
She had a good figure and wore a black helmet with
blond hair curling at the nape of her neck. Their eyes
met across the line and she smiled at him and for a
moment he didn't breathe. He was used to pretty
women smiling at him but no one had ever stopped
his breath before. Not because she was beautiful—
though she was—but because it was as if she knew
him, though he swore they had never met before.

He continued to watch her as the line inched forward. She had an air of separateness about her—not
sadness, just something that was holding her apart
from everyone else. The idea intrigued him, and he
determined to try to find out more about her.

He had to do a little maneuvering to make sure he
ended up on a chair with her, just a matter of letting
another couple go ahead of him. He waited until the
last second to slide up beside her, then waited until
the lift was in the air before he turned to her and
smiled. "Hi," he said. "My name's Dillon. It's a gorgeous day for skiing, isn't it?" Not the most origi-
nal introduction in the world, but he didn't want to
come on too strong.

"It is." She hesitated, then returned his smile. "I'm Rosie. I'm visiting from Chicago."

"Nice to meet you, Rosie from Chicago. Are you here with friends?"

"I'm by myself for the moment."

Smart woman, not revealing everything to an inquisitive stranger. "What about you?" she asked.

"I'm by myself, too." He looked around, toward the sign on the large pink and white banner draped across the midmountain restaurant, which proclaimed Brundage Is for Lovers. "I'd forgotten what day it was when I decided to come up this morning."

"I kind of feel like a unicorn on the ark," she said, but her smile took the sting out of the words.

"Hey, nothing wrong with being single," he said. He thought about adding that he was surprised someone as pretty as her was by herself, but that felt like such a line. And he had heard variations of the same often enough from his friends. As if good looks and commitment naturally went together.

"Are you from around here?" she asked.

"I live in Jasper, just north of here," he said.

"What do you do in Jasper?"

"I'm a cop." Better to get it out there—it would either relieve her fears that he was a serial killer shopping for his next victim or send her skiing off in the opposite direction as soon as possible. He had learned that not everyone was a fan of law enforcement.

Some of the tension went out of her and she angled toward him a little. "That must be interesting work."

"Jasper is a small town, so not usually that interesting." He had been involved in some exciting cases, but he wasn't one of those cops who felt the need to try to impress the people around him with his exploits. "What do you do in Chicago?"

"Nothing that interesting." She looked out at the expanse of groomed ski runs. "What's your favorite run here?"

He followed her lead into a conversation about the various skiing options. The more they talked, the more intrigued he became. Rosie had a low, contralto voice that was one of the sexiest things he had ever heard, and she was an experienced enough skier that when he suggested they try a more difficult blue run that led off from the top of the lift, she didn't hesitate.

"See you at the bottom," she said and took off, forcing him to pursue, which he didn't really mind since it afforded him a view of her skiing gracefully in front of him.

He passed her halfway down the run, but she caught up with him when they were almost to the bottom, and skied to a stop in a spray of snow, laughing. "That was wonderful," she said. "What other runs should we try?"

The smile she sent him warmed him through, in spite of temperatures in the teens. "Tell me the last book you read that you enjoyed," she said on the way up, and there followed a discussion of novels—she enjoyed historical fiction, while he confessed a preference for detective novels, which made her laugh.

"Don't authors get things wrong and ruin the book for you?" she asked.

"Not in the really good novels," he said. "Besides, I'm always hoping I'll learn something."

"Do you solve many murders in Jasper?" she asked.

"There's a first time for everything."

At noon they stopped midmountain and ate beneath the Brundage Is for Lovers banner. She removed her helmet and goggles to reveal blond waves, and eyes a deeper shade of green than his own, with long lashes. Neither of them said anything when the server wished them a Happy Valentine's Day. "It is a good day," she said when the server had gone. "Even if I'm not celebrating Saint Valentine."

He toasted her with his water glass and silently thanked whatever fates had put them in the same lift line this morning. Though he never minded skiing alone, spending the day with her was an unexpected gift.

"Do you have a last name, Rosie?" he asked over bowls of chili smothered in cheese.

"Rosie Kenley."

He set down his spoon and extended his hand. "Pleased to meet you, Rosie Kenley. I'm Dillon Diaz."

"So what is a guy like you doing alone on a day like this?" she asked. "I'd have to be blind not to notice how every woman in the place looks at you. And you seem like the type who'd have plenty of friends."

He unwrapped a packet of crackers. "I'm not involved with anyone at the moment and sometimes I prefer to ski alone."

"I'm sorry I ruined that for you," she said.

"I'm not." He spooned up chili, watching her as she ate also. "As long as we're asking nosy questions, what are you doing alone?" he hazarded after a few moments. "There are plenty of men here watching you, too."

She covered her mouth with her hand and choked back a laugh, glee dancing in her eyes. She sipped water, then sat back. "I guess I deserved that one. All right, I'll confess. I just split up with someone and the thought of staying in the city for Valentine's Day was just too much. Getting away and doing something active seemed like just the thing."

"Your ex must have been an idiot," he said.

"He is. But so was I." Her smile had faded and there was real pain behind her words, so he didn't ask for details, and she didn't volunteer any. "Do you want to keep skiing together this afternoon?" she asked. "I'll understand if you want to be alone."

"Now that I've met you, I don't want to be alone at all," he said. They spent the rest of the day together, attraction building, and when the lifts began to shut down, he was reluctant to leave her. "Do you want to have dinner?" he asked.

"Yes. I'd love that."

At dinner, she took a camera from her backpack and took a photo of him, then they took a selfie together. She leaned close to him and he put his arm around her. The perfume of her hair enveloped him as her breast pressed against his arm. "I could get used to this," he said in a low voice, and he saw the same desire he felt reflected back at him.

"I'm staying at the Grand Lodge," she said after they had battled over the check and she had reluctantly allowed him to pay. "Would you like to come back with me?"

"Yes."

They were barely though the door before they came together with a hunger that surprised him. She kissed him fiercely and he felt her need, which only made him want her more. Whoever that jerk was who broke up with her, Dillon was going to make sure she forgot about him tonight. He swept her into his arms and carried her into the bedroom. She threw back her head and laughed. "Too much of a cliché?" he asked as he stood by the bed.

She shook her head, then pulled his mouth down to hers. He fell with her onto the mattress, and together they swept half a dozen pillows from the spread and tore at each other's clothing. They weren't gentle or graceful or the least bit tentative, but oh, was it wonderful. Dillon didn't really believe in perfection, but that evening had been close to it. They had no past baggage or outside concerns to interrupt their focus on each other. Their lovemaking had been intense, intimate and magical. He had awakened beside her the next morning a little dazed—grateful and awed and unnerved by the intensity of his feelings. But he had long ago learned not to run from fear, but to ride with it and through it.

She rolled over and curled against him, her head on his shoulder. "What do you want to do today?" she asked.

"You came to ski," he said.

"I came to forget." She kissed his cheek. "You're helping with that."

They made love again, sleepily, tenderly, thoroughly. That must have been when it happened—one lucky sperm making its way to her egg because in their haste they forgot the condom. So strange to think in that moment they hadn't known what was to come.

They spent the morning making love, the afternoon exploring the town, and never made it to the ski slopes. That evening they returned to her room and watched a movie, cuddled together, before making love once more and falling asleep.

When Dillon woke Monday morning he knew she was gone before he even opened his eyes. The room was empty. Colder. He rolled over and stared at the note on hotel stationery, resting on the pillow that still bore the imprint from her hair. *Dearest Dillon. Thank you for the most wonderful weekend. I will never forget it, or you. I'm sorry I had to leave so early. I didn't want to wake you. All my best. Rosie.*

He crumpled the note and started to throw it away, throat tight with what he told himself was anger but he knew now had been grief. How many times that weekend had he started to ask for her number? But such practicalities had seemed out of place in the fantasy they were building.

He smoothed out the note and read it again. She said she would never forget him. But he needed to forget her. If she had really wanted to see him again, she would have offered her contact information. He turned the paper over to make sure nothing else was written there, but there was nothing but the hotel logo.

No, Rosie clearly meant for the weekend to be exactly what she said she needed—a break from real life. A life in which he had no place. He got up and dressed, and told himself it didn't matter. Long-distance relationships never worked out, and Chicago and Jasper were a long way apart.

But he kept the note, carefully folded and tucked into his bedside drawer at his house, where he took it out and reread it some nights when he couldn't sleep. He had started looking for her the next day, only to be frustrated by his inability to find any information about the mysterious Rosie Kenley.

And now she was here across from him. His mother, who believed in such things, would probably say the universe was bringing them together again. He didn't know about that, but he was happy to have a chance to build something between them, especially now that they had a child who would connect them forever.

Forever. A word that ought to fill him with fear but somehow didn't.

Chapter Ten

Roslyn and Dillon had coffee and protein bars for breakfast, while Bentley had the last of the kibble Dillon had packed. Not the most satisfying meal, but it would keep them going. While she repacked her belongings, he and Bentley walked down to the creek and refilled the water bottles with filtered water. He found a single boot print at the edge of the pool where he gathered water—maybe a size 10, with waffle soles. Probably made by whoever had tried to steal Roslyn's camera last night. The man in the photograph. Would he try to come after them again?

If Dillon were alone, he would show the boot print to Bentley, and order the dog to find the person who had made it. He was confident Bentley could follow the trail, barely eight hours old. But then what? The man might be armed. He might intend to harm them. Out of range of communication, with no backup and Roslyn and her unborn child to protect, Dillon couldn't risk a confrontation.

"Did you see any signs of last night's intruder?" Roslyn asked when he returned to the cave.

He hesitated, undecided how to answer her.

"I know you checked when you were out there." She slipped her daypack onto her back and shrugged to settle it on her shoulders. "You're always taking note of everything around you. I noticed it at the ski resort. I figured it was part of your law enforcement training—or did you do that even before you joined the police department?"

"I like to think I was pretty observant before." He handed her a water bottle and slipped the other into his pack. "But law enforcement training does make you hyper aware of everything that could be going on around you." Your life, and the lives of people you were sworn to protect, could depend on it.

"And you didn't answer my question," she said. "Did you see anything suspicious out there?"

"A single boot print," he admitted. "But not enough of a trail for me to follow." No need to mention Bentley. "My guess is the guy is long gone by now."

She searched his face, and he wondered if she knew he was holding back his real concern—that whoever had been tracking them since yesterday would keep following them. Or maybe he had already moved ahead of them on the trail, to find a spot where he could lie in wait to ambush them.

He glanced down at Bentley, who gazed up at him with trusting blue eyes. If the dog could talk, Dillon imagined he would say, *You can count on me to let you know if anyone is out there.* "Bentley will alert us if there's anything we need to worry about," Dillon told Roslyn. "If whoever it is is still following us, he won't know we have a secret weapon."

Her lips thinned as her mouth tightened, but no fear registered in her eyes. "I'm ready to leave when you are," she said.

"We'll take it slow," he said again, as much as a reminder to him as a reassurance for her. "And we'll rest whenever you need to. Just say the word."

"I'll be fine," she said. "I'm focusing on the prospect of a hot shower, a nap on a soft bed, and ice cream."

"Yeah. Those all sound good." Thoughts of those things would help him get through the rough stretches too—especially if he thought about enjoying them all with her.

CAMERA SHUTTERS CLICKED on all sides as Ava and Lacey passed through the crowd on the street around the police station. "Look! A police dog!" someone said.

"Isn't he gorgeous?" said someone else.

Ava resisted the urge to point out that "he" was a "she" and kept moving, though she watched the crowd out of the corner of her eye for any sign of trouble. The people filling the sidewalks and streets seemed to be a mix of tourists and media—the latter distinguished by bigger cameras, microphones and business casual clothing, while the tourists favored cell phones, shorts and T-shirts.

Lacey, as if aware of her admirers, practically pranced along the sidewalk, head up, mouth open in what Ava knew wasn't really a smile but sometimes looked like one.

"Officer, can you tell us anything about the search for Roslyn Kern?" A big man with a microphone blocked their path. Lacey sat as she had been trained, but kept her gaze fixed on the man. He noticed and took half a step back.

Ava tried for an expression that was pleasant, but stern. "I don't have any information on that," she said. "You're welcome to contact the police public information officer about that." That particular job rotated through the staff. Ava thought the current PIO was Captain Rutledge. Fitting, since he loved posing for the cameras. But he wasn't going to be any more informative about Roslyn Kern than Ava was.

"We understand one of your officers was part of the initial search for Ms. Kern and that he is now also missing," the reporter continued. "Can you tell us about him?"

Ava fixed him with the cold look she reserved for people who especially annoyed her. Beside her, Lacey tensed. Ava signaled the dog to stand down, but the reporter regarded the dog and took another step back. "Excuse me, I have work to do," Ava said and moved around him.

They headed up West Main, passed the pink awnings of the Pinup Girl Salon, then crossed over Elm. "Excuse me, Officer." A gray-haired woman with a large canvas tote stopped her. An older man in a large straw hat joined them. "Can you tell us where to find a public restroom?" the woman asked.

Ava gave them directions to the park in the center of town and they thanked her and left. Half a block farther on she helped a man with a laptop who was looking for the public library. Shortly after that, a man pulled into a no parking zone in front of Blaze's River Tours and Rafting, and Ava informed him that he would have to move or his car would be towed. He wasn't happy, but he complied, and Ava and Lacey moved on. At the alley between Millard's Diner and a T-shirt shop, Lacey began whining.

"What is it, girl?" Ava asked.

The dog looked down the alley, ears forward, forehead creased in a way that made her look worried. Ava stared down the alley, but saw nothing but the usual trash cans and stacked pallets waiting to be picked up.

Lacey looked up at her, then back down the alley, and let out a short bark. Something had the dog upset. Not alert the way she would be if pursuing a suspect, but...concerned. "Let's go see," Ava said and started cautiously down the alley, Lacey tugging at her lead.

The dog trotted straight to the set of trash cans at the diner's side door, and shoved her long snout between them. "Lacey, back!" Ava ordered, suddenly remembering that skunks sometimes raided restaurant trash cans. The last thing she wanted was to deal with a skunked dog.

Lacey obediently backed up, but she remained focused on the trash cans. She whined, and Ava was startled when a similar whine came in response. She unclipped her flashlight and crouched down to shine it into the gap between the two cans. A single brown eye stared back at her, soft and liquid. Then she glimpsed the tip of a floppy black ear.

"It's okay," she murmured, and carefully shifted one of the cans a few inches to the side.

The puppy cowered against the wall of the restaurant. Some kind of Lab-shepherd mix, Ava guessed, maybe a few months old. She squatted down and spoke softly to the dog, which looked to be in good shape, though it wore no collar. "Where did you come from, little one?" she asked.

The dog looked at her, trembling slightly.

She dug in her pocket for a treat and extended her hand, offering it. The puppy took it, wolfed it down, then moved toward her. The next thing she knew, it was pawing at her knee and licking her face. Lacey stepped forward to nudge the pup back, though very gently.

Ava picked up the dog and cradled it. Normal procedure with strays was to take them to the local animal shelter. But she knew from her work helping to evacuate families yesterday that the shelter was full up with cats, gerbils, ferrets and other non-canine pets at the moment. She looked down at the dog, whose brown eyebrows stood out against its black face. "I'm going to take you to a very nice lady," she said. "She'll know what to do with you."

THE MORNING WAS perfect for a hike. Though smoke lingered in the skies to the west, ahead of them all was clear and blue, sun warm on their skins, a pine-scented breeze moderating the temperature. Though Roslyn still carried the mask Dylan had given her, the air here was clear enough she felt safe foregoing it. She lifted her head and breathed in deeply. Even her ankle didn't hurt too badly, now that they were moving. She felt so alive and invigorated—happy in a way she had not been for a very long time.

Ahead of her, one of the reasons for her happiness strode, pack set on broad shoulders, sun glinting on his dark hair. The shadow of beard across his cheeks, visible when he turned to look back at her, only emphasized the handsome planes of his face— a face that had filled her dreams many nights since they had parted in February.

She had been desperate when she fled to Brundage Mountain. That was what the trip had felt like—not a relaxing vacation, but running away. Hiding. Valentine's was supposed to be a day for lovers, but every heart and cupid reminded her of how alone she was.

Then Dillon Diaz had slid onto the lift chair next to her and hit her with a dazzling smile and words that, if not flirtatious, definitely telegraphed his interest. She had been charmed, and relieved, too. Here was a chance to distract herself from misery. She decided to assume the role of the mysterious femme fatale. She flirted back, offering only teasing hints at her real identity. Instead of holding back against desire, she gave in and pursued him, though in truth he was never running away. She threw herself into enjoying every moment with him, whether it was skiing down the mountain, savoring a meal together or spending the night making love. She told herself that at the end of the weekend she would pop this fantasy bubble and it would all vanish, remaining only as a lovely dream she could look back on and smile.

Except that Dillon Diaz was no dreamy phantasm. He was a flesh-and-blood man who affected her much more than she wanted to admit. Back home in Chicago, he haunted her thoughts. The time they had spent together replayed in her dreams.

And the consequences of their weekend together had definitely not vanished. The day she had stared at the results of that first pregnancy test had felt like being pulled under by a tide she couldn't fight against. "Dillon." She had whispered his name. She had to get hold of him. She had to let him know.

But fear had won out over that thought. Fear and sheer inertia from having to deal with so much. She was ashamed that it had taken her five months to muster the courage to come to Jasper to find Dillon. And in the end, he had found her. Did the fact that they had come together again by chance mean anything, or was it just another odd coincidence?

Ahead of her, he stopped and called Bentley, who had been trotting down the trail before them. He turned to Roslyn. "How are you doing?" he asked.

"I'm great." She walked up to join him, then looked down toward her boots. "The ankle isn't hurting much at all today."

He nodded and scanned the area around them. Looking for the man who had followed them yesterday, she thought. "I wish I had gotten a better look at that guy," she said. At his questioning look, she added, "The one who was following us."

"I wish I knew why he wanted your camera," Dillon said. He pulled out his phone. "No signal."

"Let me check mine." She dug in her pocket and pulled out the phone, a newer model she had treated herself to when she started her new business—a tangible sign of the fresh start she was making with her life. No Signal warned a message on the screen. She tucked the phone away. "It doesn't matter," she said. "If we keep walking, we'll get to the trailhead before long, right?"

He nodded. "We should get a signal when we're closer to the parking area. I'll call ahead and have some people meet us there to check out your ankle."

"Or I could just go to a clinic in town," she said. "I really think I'm fine."

"Search and Rescue will want to declare the mission complete," he said.

The words brought her up short. "I'm a mission?"

He laughed. "That's why Bentley and I were out here in the first place, remember?"

Of course she remembered, but she hadn't thought about all the other people who were involved—a whole search and rescue team, apparently. "I'm really embarrassed now," she said. Then another thought ambushed her. "Do you think the media knows?"

"Are you worried the press followed you here to Jasper?"

"Oh, I'm sure they didn't." Interest in her had died

down in recent weeks. "I guess I'm a little paranoid, after being in the spotlight so long."

"There's a lot going on in town this weekend," he said. He offered her one of the water bottles and she took it. "No one outside of Search and Rescue is going to pay much attention to us, I'm sure."

She drank, then returned the bottle to him. "I walked around a little bit downtown before I came hiking," she said. "The town is really cute. How long have you lived here?"

"My folks moved here when I was twelve."

"And you never wanted to move some place different—a big city?"

"Oh, I talked about it some, when I was a teenager. But when it came down to where I really wanted to live and work, this area was perfect for me. I like the outdoors and there's so much to do, any time of year. Hiking and fishing in summer and fall, skiing in winter and early spring. Rafting, climbing, golf if that's your thing. It's a short drive to McCall or Boise for live music. We have good restaurants and breweries."

She laughed at his enthusiasm. "You make it sound like paradise."

"I guess to me, it is." His expression sobered. "Maybe not so much for someone from the city."

"I live in the city for my work," she said.

"Do you think you'll go back to doing radio work?" he asked. "Do you miss it?"

She shook her head. "I don't miss getting up in the middle of the night to start work at six a.m. And

I don't miss spending my weekends doing promotional events."

"You said you were ambitious. There's nothing wrong with that," he was quick to add.

She smiled down at the baby bump. "I guess now my ambitions lie elsewhere," she said. "I'm going to make a name for myself as an audiobook narrator and voice-over artist." She looked up and her eyes met his. "That's work I can do from anywhere."

The words hung between them, heavy with meaning—or no meaning at all. Was she really going to move hundreds of miles and change her life completely to be near a man who was still such a stranger to her? She could use the excuse that it would be easier for them to co-parent if they lived near each other. And Jasper looked like a wonderful place to raise children. But what happened if things didn't work out? Clearly, he was never going to leave his hometown, so she would have to pull up stakes and move again.

Was she being sensible to think this way, or a coward?

A low growl from Bentley distracted her from these whirling thoughts. Dillon was instantly alert. She stared at the dog, who was focused on something in the woods to their left. "What is it?" she whispered.

"I don't know." Dillon stepped forward, moving cautiously, his feet scarcely making a sound on the trail. "Get behind me."

It was more order than request, but she complied.

This must be what he was like in cop mode, taking charge of the situation.

Bentley growled again, a low, fierce sound that seemed out of place coming from such a fluffy, normally friendly dog. Roslyn moved past Dillon to stand behind them, staring into the darkness amid the undergrowth. She held her breath as branches shifted and moved, even though there was no wind.

Bentley barked and started forward. "Bentley, come," Dillon commanded, and the dog returned to his side, though not without a last look over his shoulder. Dillon reached back beneath his shirt and drew out a pistol. She was sure he hadn't been wearing that yesterday, but the attempted theft of her camera must have unsettled him enough that he felt the need to be armed. "Who's there?" he shouted. "I'm a police officer. Come out with your hands where I can see them."

A crashing in the underbrush, and then a mule deer buck appeared between the trees. It stared at them a mesmerizing moment, then bounded off, away from them.

Roslyn let out the breath she had been holding and Dillon replaced the pistol in its holster at the small of his back. Bentley wagged his tail and grinned up at them both. "I should have realized he was barking at wildlife," Dillon said and bent to pat the dog. "I know his different barks by now."

"We're both a little on edge, I think." She rested a hand on his shoulder, calmed by the solid strength of him.

He nodded and straightened. "Are you ready to go on?" he asked.

"Yes. The sooner we get off this trail, the better." It was beautiful here, but for now she had enjoyed all the wildness she could handle.

Chapter Eleven

Brady told himself he should forget about Kent Anderson and let the US Marshals handle the search, but the knowledge that someone they couldn't identify was out there in the area where at least some people seemed to think Anderson might be nagged at him all during his morning patrol. When he returned to the station at lunchtime he sought out Margaret Avery. A tall woman with a sweep of long brown hair, the lieutenant was acknowledged as the force's best detective. "Do you have a minute to talk?" Brady asked.

"Sure." She swiveled her chair away from her computer to face him. "What's up?"

He sat in the visitor's chair in front of her desk and leaned closer. "What do you think of the marshal's theory that Kent Anderson is headed to Nevada?"

"I was just reading through the transcript of the interviews the McCall detectives did with Deena Marquette and Sean Tyson." She nodded at her computer screen. "I asked Eli to send them over."

"Did they say anything about Nevada?" Brady asked.

"No. They said Anderson asked for warm clothes and boots. Their impression was he intended to head north. They claimed not to know where at first, then admitted Anderson had talked about going to Alaska."

"So that doesn't exactly contradict the guy who told the marshals Anderson was headed to Nevada. Anderson talked about Alaska, but maybe he decided on Nevada instead."

"No, but we also have the statement from the driver who dropped off the hitchhiker two blocks from the Williams Gap Trailhead," she said. "He was clear on his description of the man and identified Anderson from a photo lineup."

"That seems pretty definite," Brady said.

"But apparently the marshals discounted it," Margaret said.

"Deputy Rand said they thought Marquette and Tyson were lying, but they apparently believed the other guy they talked to. Do we know anything about him?"

She read from the notebook open in front of her. "Donald Aldeen, twenty-four, an auto mechanic in Yellow Pine. He and Kent Anderson apparently did attend the same elementary school. That's all I've been able to find out so far, but I think we'll be hearing more from Mr. Aldeen soon."

"Oh?" Brady sat up straighter. Margaret's expression, while not exactly smug, did hint that she knew something significant. "Why do you say that?"

"I got a call this morning from a reporter I know

with the *Idaho Statesman*. She and I have known each other for years and she wanted to pick my brain about the hunt for Kent Anderson. I told her I couldn't tell her anything that hadn't already been in the news, but in the course of our conversation, she told me something interesting."

Brady waited. Margaret leaned toward him across the desk. "She said their newsroom got a call this morning from someone named Donald Aldeen who claimed to be Kent Anderson's best friend. He said he could give them the whole scoop on Anderson— for a hefty fee."

"He wanted to sell the story?"

"Exactly. The *Statesman* turned him down flat. They don't pay for news. But they also did a little research of their own and they couldn't find any indication that Anderson and this guy were all that close. None of the other people they talked to who knew Anderson remembered him hanging out with Aldeen. My friend said she's seen this before— people on the periphery of the story who claim a close relationship to the people involved, hoping to gain money or fame or just attention."

"And she thinks Aldeen falls into that category?"

"She does."

"So he made up the whole thing about Nevada?"

Margaret sat back. "I don't know. But he obviously convinced the marshals."

"He told them what they wanted to hear," Brady said.

"Could be," Margaret said. "In any case, my

friend is going to dig some more into his background and her paper may run a story. At the very least, she agreed to share with me what she learns."

"What do we do in the meantime?"

"We ask the firefighters and others in the area to keep a lookout for Anderson and we try to get word to Dillon."

"He probably isn't in any danger," Brady said. "But still…"

"But still." Margaret nodded. "Dillon is one of ours, and we protect our own, no matter what the marshals say."

BY THE TIME Ava and the stray pup arrived, things were a little calmer at Daniels Canine Academy than they had been the day before. Or rather, the crowd of people milling about was smaller, and fewer cars clogged the driveway and parking area. But the air was filled with the sounds of dogs—barking, whining, yipping and howling. Emma raised her voice to be heard over the cacophony. "Hello, Ava." She bent to greet Lacey. "And hello, Lacey."

Lacey wagged her tail in greeting to one of her favorite people. Emma patted the dog, then straightened and zeroed in on the pup in Ava's arms. "Who is this?"

"I was hoping you'd know." Ava handed over the wriggling pup. Emma cuddled the pup—a male, Ava had determined—and stroked its fuzzy head.

"I don't recognize him," Emma said. She examined the dog, running her hands along its body and looking in its mouth. "He's about ten weeks old, I'd guess. He looks well cared for."

"I found him behind some garbage cans in the alley next to Millard's Diner," Ava said. "Or rather, Lacey found him."

"Good girl," Emma addressed Lacey, who thumped her tail in response.

"Can you keep him here while I search for his owners?" Ava said. "The regular animal shelter is full up with evacuees' pets."

"Of course," Emma said. "Even better, if you have time we can run him over to Tashya and have her check for a microchip. We have a scanner in our little on-site clinic."

"I have time. Do you think a pup this young would be chipped?"

"It depends. Most shelters chip them before they put them up for adoption, and some breeders, too, though I doubt this little guy is anything but a hundred percent mutt."

Ava scratched the pup's chin. "A really cute mutt," she said.

"Let's go see if Tashya can find anything." Emma, still cradling the puppy, led the way across the compound, Lacey and Ava in her wake. "Between random fireworks, houses full of strangers and the chaos of the fire, maybe he just escaped his backyard," Emma said as they walked.

She pushed open a door marked with a red cross. Tashya Pratt's attractive round face spread into a wide grin when she saw Ava. "Hey, there," she said.

Her light brown eyes shifted to the pup in Emma's arms. "And who is this cutie?"

"I found him in the alley between the café and a T-shirt shop," Ava said. "I brought him here because the shelter is full."

"Let's check him with the scanner." Emma set the wriggling pup on the steel examination table.

"Sure thing." Tashya tucked a lock of shoulder-length, straightened black hair behind one ear, then rummaged in a deep drawer and pulled out a white plastic rectangle about the size of a cell phone. She switched it on and passed it over the dog's body, pausing at the neck. Her smile widened once again. "We're in luck." She read the information on the scanner's screen. "Looks like this little guy was adopted from McPaws shelter in McCall. We can call them, give them this code number, and they'll tell us who adopted the pup from them."

"Thanks, Tashya," Ava said.

"We can make the call for you," Emma said. "The owners can pick him up here. I know you've probably got your hands full, with everything going on in town this weekend."

"It is pretty busy," Ava said. She turned to Tashya. "And speaking of busy, how are the wedding preparations coming?"

"There's so much to do!" Tashya said. "Even for a simple wedding like ours. But it's kind of fun, too, picking out what I want. And Jason's been a big help."

"We're all looking forward to the wedding," Ava

said. The resort in McCall that Tashya and her hus-band-to-be, rookie officer Jason Wright, had chosen was gorgeous, and had a reputation for good food.

"Jason did suggest we elope to Vegas or some-place," Tashya said. "But I told him I hadn't waited four years to marry him to do it without all the peo-ple who are important to me there." She sent a fond look to Emma, who had taken Tashya in when the girl was fourteen and very lost. Emma had recog-nized Tashya's love for animals and steered her into vet tech school and the career she loved, working with Emma at Daniels Canine Academy.

Ava rubbed the dog's ears and he rolled over on the table and gnawed at her fingers. "Somebody is probably missing you," Ava said.

"How are Eli and Bear?" Tashya asked.

"They're both great." Ava couldn't help but smile when she thought of her handsome boyfriend and his goofy Newfoundland who, despite weighing in at a hundred pounds, insisted on being a lapdog. "Eli stopped by the station this morning to give us an update on a missing fugitive."

Emma nodded. "I caught a news report last night. I remember when he killed all those people at ISU. Horrible. Why would he come to a place like Jas-per?"

"He's familiar with the area. The US Marshals think he intends to hike cross-country to Nevada. But other people say he's headed to Alaska, starting from here. Local fire spotters saw a lone camper in the area around Williams Gap Trail last night—but you didn't hear that from me."

"Any word yet from Dillon?" Emma asked.

"He sent Brady a text saying he and Roslyn Kern were spending the night in those caves up above Cow Creek. They plan to walk out today."

"That's a relief," Emma said.

"How are the evacuees?" Ava asked. A particularly plaintive howl interrupted her. "It sounds like some of them aren't settling in so well."

"A bit of separation anxiety," Emma said. "Dogs are very sensitive and they pick up on stress in the people they care about. They'll be happier in a couple of days when they're back to their regular routines. Some people have already stopped by to reclaim their pets and take them to wherever they've found to stay until they're allowed back into their homes."

"I heard about the incident with Captain Rutledge and the poodle," Ava said.

Emma's expression grew fierce. "When he drew his weapon, I was so angry I was looking around for something to hit him over the head with," she said. "Though I doubt that would have knocked any sense into him."

"The captain just doesn't like dogs," Ava said.

"I think he's afraid of them," Tashya said.

Ava and Emma stared at her. Tashya shrugged. "You see it sometimes. People avoid dogs because they're afraid of them, sometimes because they've been bitten or had a frightening encounter, maybe when they were a kid. Sometimes it's because they haven't spent time around dogs and don't know how wonderful they can be."

"You could be right," Emma said. "But that's no excuse for violence."

"Of course not," Ava said. "Maybe teaching him how to interact with dogs will help."

"Word gets around fast, I see," Emma said. "Though I guess I'm not surprised."

"We all think the training program is a great idea," Ava said. "Let me know if you need any help."

"I might take you up on that," Emma said. "If I can get Arthur to really come to the training, I'm thinking about offering similar classes to other law enforcement people in the area. Fire departments, paramedics and EMTs, too. Knowing how to deal with an upset dog when they arrive at an emergency situation would make life easier and safer for everyone."

"That's a terrific idea," Tashya said.

"I will need help." Emma picked up the puppy once more and looked down at Lacey, who had settled onto her side on the floor. "Lacey could help, too," she said. "Police dogs like her can look really scary. She would be great for demonstrations."

"Count me in. Eli and Bear could help, too." Ava checked her watch. "It's been great talking to you, but I should go."

"It was good talking to you, too. And don't worry about this little fellow. I'll take care of him."

Ava and Lacey walked back out to the police cruiser, where they were hailed by a harried-looking woman with two small girls in tow. "Excuse me!" the woman called as Ava approached the cruiser. "Are you the officer who picked up the puppy in town? Someone told me they saw a police officer with a puppy."

"Are you missing your dog?" Ava asked.

"Where is Bruno?" one of the little girls wailed. Beside her, her sister burst into tears.

"He's mostly black, with brown eyebrows and two brown paws," the woman said. "We brought him to town with us because we were afraid if the fire shifted we might not be able to get back into our house, but when I opened the car door to help the girls out of their booster seats, he got out of the car and ran down the street. We've been looking all over for him and someone said they thought they saw a woman police officer with him. Then someone else told us you might have brought him here."

"Let's go see," Ava said.

The woman and her daughters followed Ava back to the clinic. Tashya looked up at their approach. "I think we've found the pup's owner," Ava said.

"Emma took him to her office," Tashya said.

Ava led the woman and her daughters to the office where Emma had placed the stray pup in a carrier next to her desk. She looked up when they entered, and set aside the phone she had been holding. "Do you have Bruno?" the woman asked, worry lines etched on her face.

"I think the pup I found belongs to this family," Ava said. "They've been searching for him."

Emma opened the kennel and the pup tumbled out. "Bruno!" the girls shrieked, and fell to their knees to wrestle with the puppy, who yipped joyously and licked their faces.

"Thank you for taking care of him," the woman said. She brushed at her eyes, then offered her hand. "I'm Kaitlyn Elwood," she said. "I was telling the officer that Bruno got out of our car when we came to town to run errands. We normally leave him at home in his crate, but we were afraid to do that in case the police decided to close off our neighborhood and not let us back in."

"Where do you live?" Ava asked.

"Off County Road 14. Our place backs up to the national forest. The last I heard, the fire wasn't threatening our area, but I've lived here long enough to know how quickly that can change."

"I know that neighborhood," Emma said. "You're not far from the Cow Creek Loop."

"That's right," Kaitlyn said. "We occasionally see hikers who have gotten off the trail. My husband is thinking about putting up some signposts to send them off our property and back in the right direction. I saw a guy this morning. I yelled at him that he was going the wrong way and he just glared at me." She shrugged. "There's no accounting for some people."

"There shouldn't be anyone on the trail right now," Ava said. "There's a big sign at the trailhead that says the trail is closed because of the fire."

"This guy was there," Kaitlyn said. "He had a big

backpack and everything. Maybe he's one of those people who think the rules don't apply to them."

Maybe. But Ava's intuition told her there was something more. "What did he look like?" she asked.

"Average height and weight. He wore a cap so I couldn't tell much about his hair, but it was short. Khaki pants and a black T-shirt. A big backpack—that camo green."

Ava took out a notebook and wrote all this down. "Would you recognize him if you saw him again?" she asked.

The woman rubbed her mouth. "Well, I don't know. I only saw him for a few seconds." She lowered her hand and nodded. "But yeah, I think so, just because he stopped and gave me such a glare." She shuddered. "Why? Is something wrong?"

Ava didn't answer that question. "What's your phone number, in case we have more questions?" she asked.

The woman rattled off a number, glanced at her children, who were still wrestling with the puppy, then back at Ava. She lowered her voice. "Do I need to be worried about something?"

"No. But if you see the man again, don't interact with him at all. Call 911 and tell them I said to contact the police department." Ava took a business card from her wallet and handed it to the woman. "And call me if you have any questions or concerns."

The woman nodded and tucked the card away. "Come on, girls," she said. "We need to get Bruno home." She took a leash from her purse and snapped it onto the dog's collar. "And he's not going to get away this time."

Emma said nothing until the woman and her family were gone. "Do you think the man she saw is Kent Anderson?" she asked.

"I don't know," Ava said. She reread the man's description. It fit that of Kent Anderson and the clothes he had on the last time he was seen, but a lot of men probably matched those slim details. "I need to tell the chief."

"If it is him," Emma said, "he's not that far from the caves, where Dillon and Roslyn Kern are supposed to have spent the night."

Ava nodded. It was close. Too close for comfort.

Chapter Twelve

Roslyn did not want to think about her throbbing ankle, aching back, burning indigestion or sunburned nose. The energy and optimism of the morning had faded, and the miles were catching up with her. The pleasant breeze had died, the heat had intensified, and the thought of eating one more protein bar—the only food they had left—made her feel slightly nauseous. But she was determined to keep going. She wasn't going to complain, not when Dillon was marching on ahead of her and didn't appear the least bit tired or sore.

Why had she ever been worried about seeing him again? Clearly, she had stunned him with the news that she was carrying his baby, but he had recovered from the shock quickly enough. He seemed sincere about wanting to be involved in his future son or daughter's life. That was all good—right?

She wanted to believe so, but things had seldom worked out for her the way she hoped they would. What if they didn't agree about the best way to raise a child? What if he became interested in someone else and they married and he started another family? Last night in her arms she had believed they might have a future together, but they had had a wonderful weekend together before and said goodbye easily enough. At least, he had given no indication at the time that he wanted to see her again. Maybe he didn't think of her in terms of a long-term relationship, only someone he could enjoy in the moment. Would he abandon her and their child when someone better came along?

Why was she worrying about all this right now?

Maybe because as much as she liked Dillon, they still didn't know each other that well. He glanced back at her and stopped. "Are you okay?" he asked. "Do you need to stop?"

She opened her mouth to protest that she was fine, then decided to tell the truth. "I'm pretty tired," she said. "I could use a break."

He looked around, then led her to a grouping of boulders in the shade of a clump of aspen. It wasn't a cushioned easy chair, but she welcomed the chance to take a load off her aching feet and swollen ankle.

Dillon sat beside her and carefully lifted her injured foot into his lap. He massaged it gently. "I know it hurts," he said. "But I don't think you're doing any permanent damage."

"What you're doing right now feels great," she said. She closed her eyes and sighed. Every time he touched her felt great. Which made it difficult to think clearly when he was near. She wanted to lose herself in the moment, but she told herself she should be doing more to get to know him better.

"How did you get into search and rescue work?" she asked. "Was that before or after you became a cop?"

"After." He continued to massage her ankle, fingers strong but gentle. "I really did it to work with Bentley. I had friends with police dogs and it just seemed like working one-on-one with an animal like that would be really special. But I thought I'd prefer search and rescue. And I was right. Bentley has been great, and I've learned a lot."

"So I guess you're trained in first aid?"

He nodded. "And white water rescue and climbing and avalanche rescue—all the skills to address the kind of rescues we're called on to do here. Bentley doesn't even come with me on some calls, though neither one of us likes that much."

The dog sat beside Dillon and leaned against his leg. Dillon reached down to scratch his ears. "Do you have any pets?" he asked.

"No. I had a dog when I was a girl—Pepper. He was a little brown dog, maybe part Chihuahua." She smiled, remembering.

"You could get a dog now," he said. "Especially since you're working at home."

"Maybe after the baby is older," she said. "That might be nice." She searched for a way to direct the conversation back to him. There was so much she wanted to know—needed to know. "You said you

moved to Jasper when you were twelve?" she asked.
"Where did you live before that?"

"Denver. It was a big adjustment, coming from the
big city, but it didn't take me long to make friends
and settle in." His smile radiated the happiness behind those words.

She could believe that. Dillon was so charming
and friendly he could easily be the most popular person in any room. "Does your family still live here?"
she asked.

"Oh, yes. My dad owns a construction company.
My mom manages his office—and she tries to manage me and my two brothers."

"Are you the youngest?"

"Oldest." He grinned. "And according to her, I
am long overdue to get married and give her grand-
children." His gaze dropped to her abdomen. "She is
going to be over the moon about this baby."

Roslyn's chest felt full of butterflies. "Is she going
to be upset that we're not married?"

"A little disappointed, maybe, but my mom isn't
judgmental."

"Do you think she'll like me?"

"She'll love you." He moved his hands from her
ankle to her shoulders. "Don't worry. Mom can be
a bit overwhelming at first—she has a big personality. But I know she's going to love you. How could
she not?"

Lots of people in her life had managed not to
love her, Roslyn thought. She could imagine a dot-
ing mother not being pleased to meet the woman

who had ended up pregnant by her son as the result of a weekend fling.

"What about your parents?" Dillon asked. "Where do they live?"

"My mom is in Shreveport, Louisiana, and my dad is in Alaska. They divorced when I was three and they've both remarried a couple of times since then."

"Are they excited about the baby?"

Her mother's first words upon hearing the news were "I hope you're not counting on me for help with this kid." Her father had been kinder. "That's great, honey. You'll have to come up here so I can meet my newest grandchild after he's born." No offer to come see her—she hadn't laid eyes on her father in at least ten years. "My parents are really busy with their own lives," she said.

Dillon nodded, and she could practically see him processing this statement. Such a different response from what he expected from his own mother. It sounded like his family was still close. Would that make him a better dad? "My mom will do anything she can for you and that baby," he said. "She'll be thrilled, but if she gets too overbearing, don't be afraid to tell her to back off. She hears it from me all the time, and mostly, she's good about reining herself in."

You're her darling boy, Roslyn thought. *She would probably forgive you anything. I'm some stranger who dropped into her life unexpectedly.*

There she went, being pessimistic again. The last few months, since learning about the baby, she had been trying to nurture a more positive attitude. She couldn't control what happened in the future, only how she reacted. For her child's sake, she wanted to focus on the positive. "Where do you live?" she asked. "Do you have an apartment? A house?"

"I bought a house last year. I saw how real estate prices were soaring and figured I'd better get something while I could still afford it. I've done some remodeling to fix it up how I wanted it. It's nice, having a place of my own."

"What's it like?"

"Three bedrooms, two baths. Two acres with some trees. It's about three miles north of town."

"That's a big place for a single guy."

"I bought it with the future in mind."

The words sent a hot shiver through her. What was that supposed to mean? But she wasn't sure she was ready to hear the answer.

Instead, she turned her attention to the dog. Bentley wagged his tail at her, then resumed watching Dillon. "He seems very devoted," she said.

"Aussies are very loyal," he said. "But he likes pretty much everyone. It's a good quality in a rescue dog. You don't want a lost child running the other direction because a fierce-looking dog is coming after them. Bentley is so gentle he doesn't frighten people, though he can be protective when he needs to be."

"He chased off that intruder last night," she said.

"He'll let us know if anyone is out there," Dillon said.

"Or any deer." She laughed, remembering her relief at their earlier encounter.

"I've been watching him and he hasn't picked up on anyone or anything else," Dillon said. "Maybe the guy who was after your camera decided he'd be better off leaving."

"I hope so," she said. "Though I wish I knew who it was."

"I'd like to take another look at that photo you took," he said.

She fished the camera from her pack, switched it on and handed it to him. He studied the figure for a long time, then returned the camera to her. "Do you recognize him?" he asked.

"No."

"Take a good look. Does he look familiar at all?"

She focused on the photo, but nothing about the figure in it was familiar. "No." She shook her head. "Does he look familiar to you?"

He sat back. "No. I'm just trying to figure out who would be following us. Do you think someone in your life in Chicago would follow you to Jasper? Maybe a reporter trying to get a scoop? You said the media have been harassing you."

"They have, but like I said, a lot of that has died down in the last few weeks. And following me to another state is pretty extreme. It's not like anyone outside of Chicago even knows who I am. Really, I think the only reason the local press picked up the story and ran with it was because the station I worked for made such a big deal about my engagement to Matt."

"Rockin' Roz and Mad Matt." He scowled.

She sighed. "I wanted to keep my private life private, but the station manager and Matt both pushed for using the relationship to build ratings. The next thing I knew, there were billboards and ads in the paper. I was waiting to cross the street one afternoon and a city bus went by with my face plastered across the back." She shuddered at the memory.

"What happened after you broke off the engagement?" he asked.

"Oh, they tried to milk that, too. I had to hire a lawyer to prevent them from using my image in more ads. I think station management probably paid some reporters to keep my name in the paper and on local TV, though I could never prove it."

"Could Matt or the station have sent someone to follow you here?" Dillon asked.

She shook her head. "There's no need. Matt has a new girlfriend now. Her name is Dorothy, but on-air she's D-Licious. Matt didn't waste any time, making a move on her. I've been so tempted to call her up and tell her she's probably just another way for Matt to improve his chances of moving on to bigger and better things, but she probably wouldn't believe me. I wouldn't have if someone had tried to warn me."

"Does Matt know about the baby?" Dillon asked. "Would he wonder if it was his?"

She put a protective hand on her abdomen. "The baby isn't his. Definitely not."

"I believe you, but he might jump to the wrong conclusion, or not know how far along you are."

"No. Matt made it very clear he did not want children," she said. "I think that was real, not part of the publicity stunt."

As if knowing they were talking about it, the baby moved inside her. "I've always wanted children," she said.

"Me, too," he said.

"Really?"

"Really. Do you find that hard to believe?"

"Most men I've dated were ambivalent at best," she said. "They saw fatherhood as some far-off possibility, not a cherished reality."

"I bought my house with the idea that I'd have a family there," he said. "When I found the right partner."

He didn't touch her with his hands, but the look in his eyes was a caress. She swallowed the lump of emotion that rose in her throat. They had known each other such a short time. How could they know they were right for each other?

"I really don't think the person in that photo has anything to do with me," she said. "What about you? You're a cop. Maybe he's following you."

"I wasn't anywhere near here until I was sent to find you," he said.

"Maybe he saw you and recognized you," she said. "You might have made enemies."

"I probably have, but I don't know this man."

"Then maybe he's just another lost hiker," she said. "He's following us, hoping we'll lead him to safety."

Dillon shook his head. "If that's the case, why not say something? Why not ask for help, or to hike with us? Why try to steal your camera?"

"You're right." She stared at the man in the photo again. Just a blurred image, no features distinguishable. "I'm sure I don't know him," she said. "Maybe we'll never know why he's out there. I hope we never find out."

"I hope we do," Dillon said. "He's caused us enough trouble already. I'd just as soon arrest him for attempted theft and be done with him."

She supposed cops saw so many situations in terms of right and wrong, legal and illegal. They saw one correct way to deal with a situation. She rubbed her belly. So much of life was too complicated for those kinds of solutions. "How much farther to town?" she asked.

"Three more miles."

"How long will that take?"

He considered the question, either because he needed to calculate the time, or because he was trying to think of a diplomatic way to tell her they were traveling very slowly. But she already knew that. She had been a swift hiker before, but pregnancy and a sprained ankle slowed her down considerably.

"Not more than two hours," Dillon said.

Two hours didn't sound like so long. *And then what?* she wondered. How would she and Dillon work out how to parent a child together while remaining apart?

Don't obsess about the future, she reminded herself. *Focus on right now.* Right now, she needed to keep putting one foot in front of the other, walking her way out of one predicament, without angsting over problems that hadn't happened yet.

At fifty, Colleen Diaz still turned heads, especially among men of a certain age—though those familiar with her husband, Ramon, and her three sons, who included Jasper Police Sergeant Dillon Diaz, didn't overtly stare, in case one of the men in her life took offense. Colleen was well aware of the effect she had on men, and dressed to impress in tasteful but stylish clothes that played up her generous curves and creamy skin. She wore her hair long, the red color still vibrant, and she held her head up high and looked people in the eye when she spoke to them.

Chief Doug Walters was the focus of Colleen's clear hazel gaze at the moment. "What are you doing to rescue my son?" she asked. She had cornered the chief in the squad room, where everyone who happened to be in the station pretended to be working. But Walters knew they were all avidly attuned to this conversation. Dillon's mother had a reputation as a woman who didn't take no for an answer. Her charm, beauty and refusal to back down had reportedly contributed to the fact that Diaz Construction had never had a client fail to pay them. If a payment was late, Colleen personally called upon the client and persuaded them to hand over the money.

But Walters had never expected to find himself the focus of Colleen's attention. "Dillon doesn't need rescuing, Mrs. Diaz," he said. "We expect him back sometime today."

"I'm sure Dillon would tell you that," Colleen said. "Never mind that he's trapped by a wildfire and there's an escaped killer running around out there."

Colleen had obviously been listening to the news accounts, which had half the town fearful of being killed in their beds by Kent Anderson, despite the fact that the marshals believed Anderson to be in Nevada and local law enforcement hadn't been able to gather evidence to prove otherwise. "Dillon texted yesterday that he's safe and he's in no danger from the fire or anything else." Walters did his best to look stern, but Colleen's laser gaze made him feel several inches shorter.

"What do you know about this woman he's with?" Colleen asked.

"Roslyn Kern?" Walters furrowed his brow, trying to recall what he knew about the woman Dillon had rescued. "I believe she's from Chicago."

"Yes, and she's pregnant, and was on the radio. Who is the father of her baby and why isn't he here?"

Walters wanted to ask her why she was asking him if she knew so much about Roslyn Kern. But he didn't dare. "I don't know about the baby's father," he said. "But that's really none of my concern."

"I saw her picture. She's very pretty. Close to Dillon's age." She tilted her head, considering. "He's bound to make an impression on her—such a strong, handsome man, rescuing her from danger."

Walters stared. Was she imagining a romance between this woman and Sergeant Diaz? He remained silent, but Colleen wasn't having it. "What do you think?" she asked. "Would this woman be good for Dillon?"

"I've never met the woman," he said. "And I don't interfere in my officers' personal lives."

"None of the local women seem to suit him," she said. "But I know he's ready to settle down. He bought that big house that's perfect for a family."

Walters winced inwardly. Dillon's fellow officers were never going to let him live this down.

Colleen narrowed her eyes. "You say you've had a text from him? He hasn't answered any of my messages."

Walters wasn't even going to go there. "I'm sure you don't have anything to worry about, Mrs. Diaz," he said. "Your son is an experienced officer and a trained search and rescue team member. He's well equipped and prepared for any situation."

"You don't have any children, do you, Chief?" she asked.

"No, I don't."

"Then you can't understand a parent's worry." She leaned toward him and he fought not to lean away. "When you talk to Dillon, you tell him to call his mother."

"Yes, ma'am."

"Chief?" Teresa approached. "You have a call on line one. I forwarded it to your office."

"Excuse me, Mrs. Diaz." Walters nodded goodbye and moved past her, toward his office.

"Let me show you out," Teresa said, taking Colleen's arm.

He was holding the silent receiver in his hand when Teresa appeared in his doorway a few moments later. "There was no call," Walters said.

"There wasn't," she admitted. "But you looked like you needed rescuing."

He ought to be insulted by this, but could only return Teresa's grin. She had blue eyes, and they were less intimidating than Colleen's. "Thanks. I'd heard stories about Dillon's mom but never interacted with her one-on-one. She's definitely a force to be reckoned with."

Teresa moved further into the office. "Every organization in town knows if you need a job done, get Colleen Diaz on your committee. And she is a real mama bear when it comes to her boys. They're all three spoiled rotten, but it hasn't ruined them."

A knock on the doorframe turned their attention to the door, where Ava stood, Lacey at her side. "Excuse me, Chief," she said. "I was out at DCA and learned something you should know."

"Come in, Ava," he said. Teresa nodded to Ava and slipped out the door as Ava moved to stand in front of Walters's desk. "What's on your mind?"

"I found a stray puppy and took it to Emma Daniels. The owner of the dog turned out to be Kaitlyn Elwood. She lives out County Road 14, on property that backs up to the national forest. She came to claim the dog and while we were talking she mentioned that she saw a man crossing her property this morning. She said something to him to direct him back to the Cow Creek Loop, which runs near there. She said he just glared at her." She pulled her notebook from her pocket and read from a page. "She described the man as average height and weight, his hair covered by a cap. He wore khaki pants, a black T-shirt, and had a camouflage backpack. That matches the description I saw for Kent Anderson."

Walters nodded. "That matches with the report from the fire spotter of someone camping in the vicinity."

"That isn't far at all from the caves where we think Dillon and Roslyn Kern spent the night," she said.

"Dillon and Ms. Kern should be hiking back toward town by now," he said. "Depending on how fast they're able to hike with Ms. Kern's injury, they should be here early afternoon, or sooner."

"I'd like permission to hike out with Lacey to meet them," Ava said. "That way he'd have backup if Kent Anderson is following him."

It wasn't a terrible idea, but it put an officer in uniform on the scene. Anderson probably didn't know Dillon was a law enforcement officer, but he wouldn't mistake Ava, in uniform and with a police K-9, for anything else. Even out of uniform, someone alone on a closed trail might raise suspicion. "I can't spare you right now," Walters said. "The situation in town is too volatile, with the crowds of tourists and media, the fire and the news hyping the stories of both Roslyn Kern and Kent Anderson. I need every officer available to quell any problems that arise."

Ava pressed her lips together, clearly unhappy with this news, but too disciplined to argue.

Walters's phone beeped. He held up one finger to indicate she should wait while he answered the summons. "Walters," he said into the receiver.

"Jenny Dix from Dispatch, Captain," said a pleasant female voice. "We just had a 911 call about a fight at the corner of West Main and South Maple. That's practically in front of the police station."

"We'll get right on it. Thanks, Jenny." He hung up the phone and looked up at Ava. "Speaking of problems, we've got a report of a fight right outside." He heaved himself out of his chair. "Let's go see what we're dealing with."

Chapter Thirteen

The two combatants were young, fit and drunk, despite the fact that it wasn't yet noon. They grappled with each other in the middle of the sidewalk, staggering around and taking turns landing blows while onlookers shouted and cheered. A television news crew even filmed from the sidelines.

Ava and the chief dragged the men apart, Ava twisting one man's arm behind his back in a painful hold that rendered him helpless. She fastened cuffs on his wrists and pointed to the curb. "Sit!" she ordered.

"I don't want to sit," he said. "That guy made a move on my girlfriend and I want to knock his head off."

"Sit or my partner will make you sit."

The man looked toward the chief, who was cuffing the other combatant. "That old man?" he sneered.

"No. This partner." She signaled to Lacey, who stepped forward and uttered a low growl.

The man's face paled. "Don't let it bite me," he said.

"Then sit."

He sat, still focused on the dog. "Call it off," he said.

At a hand signal, Lacey sat, too. She was relaxed, but her gaze was fixed on the man. She would keep him out of the way while Ava helped disperse the crowd.

"...reporting live from Jasper, Idaho, where local police have just quelled an altercation on the street in front of the police department." A handsome man with a boyish face and broad shoulders in a tan sport coat moved into Ava's line of sight, a second man with a shoulder-mount camera tracking his movement. "Officer, can you tell me if this altercation had anything to do with either the disappearance of Roslyn Kern or the search for fugitive Kent Anderson?"

"No comment," Ava said. "And you need to shut off that camera and leave now."

"This is a public street," the man said. "We have a right to be here, reporting the news as it happens."

This last sounded to Ava like the tagline for the station he worked for. "This is a crime scene and you need to leave," she said. "Or I could arrest you for interfering with an officer in the performance of her duty."

The man stared, and for a moment he thought he was going to push his luck, but at the last moment, he turned to the cameraman. "Shut it off, Mike," he said. "Let's go see what we can find on the other side of the street."

Half an hour later, when the two combatants were safely locked in cells in the basement of the police department, Ava headed back upstairs to deal with the paperwork. She was sitting at her desk when Teresa called. "I have a couple here who say they need to talk to a police officer. Could you interview them?"

"Sure. Did they say what it's about?"

"No. But they look very nervous."

"I'll come out to meet them."

Margery and Michael Blake were one of those couples who resembled each other, with short white hair cut in no particular style, soft features and pale brown eyes. "Could we talk somewhere private?" Michael asked after Ava had introduced herself and gotten their names. "What I have to say is important, but kind of sensitive." He looked around him, shoulders hunched as if ready to ward off a beating.

"Sure. Come with me." Ava led them to one of the interview rooms—a small, square space with everything painted gray—gray industrial carpet, gray walls and gray table and chairs. She caught sight of Brady as she moved down the hall and motioned for him to come with her. "This is Lieutenant Nichols," she said. "He'll be sitting in on our interview."

She went through the formalities, notifying them that their statement was being recorded and reciting their names, address and the fact that they were here voluntarily for the tape. Then she settled across from them at the table, while Brady remained by the door. "What do you have to tell us?" she asked.

The couple exchanged looks. Michael cleared his throat, then said, "Kent Anderson is our nephew."

"By marriage," Margery added. "Not blood. He didn't grow up around us. He grew up in Ketchum and just visited sometimes in summer."

Ava glanced at Brady. They were both more alert now. "Do you know where your nephew is right now?" she asked.

"No." Michael shook his head. "If we did, we'd tell you. We think it's terrible what he did. We're here because we just found out his mother's people decided to help him."

"They were bragging about it," Margery said. "I know you already talked to Deena and Sean, but there are others involved."

"The whole clan is bad news," Michael said. "When our Joe married Kent's mother, Helen, I knew the family was trouble, but I never expected something like this."

"Was there something specific you wanted us to know?" Ava asked, wanting to derail this rant. It was no news to their department that Anderson's relatives didn't always respect the law, but you couldn't prosecute people for having a bad attitude.

Margery leaned across the table toward them. "We ran into some of Helen's relatives this morning while we were shopping and Michael asked them about Kent."

"We'd seen the news reports," Michael said. "One of them said Kent had family in the area who might have aided his escape. I came right out and asked them if they had helped that murderer and they said they had. Laughed about it." He twisted his face in a look of disgust.

"Thank you for letting us know," Ava said. "What are the names of the people you talked to?"

They gave her the names of four people, all known to them, all probably already questioned by federal authorities, but it didn't hurt to have someone else confirm their involvement with Anderson.

"Do you know a man named Donald Aldeen?" Brady asked.

Margery made a face of distaste. "We know who he is," she said. "But he's someone we try to avoid."

"He's been telling people he and Kent are best friends," Brady said.

Margery looked to her husband, who shook his head. "I don't think so," he said. "I mean, they may have played together some when they were kids, but I never heard Kent or anyone who knew him well mention anybody by that name."

"Donald Aldeen told the US Marshals Service that Kent was headed to Nevada."

"What would he want in Nevada?" Michael asked. "The only place anyone mentioned to us was Alaska. He figured he could change his name and get lost up there—all that empty land and people who mind their own business. That's what they told us."

"Maybe Kent has friends in Nevada," Ava said. "Or he's been there before?"

"I don't know," Margery said. "Like we said, we weren't close to him or anything."

"Is there anything else you want to tell us?" Ava asked.

"Yes," Michael said. "The whole reason we came here was to tell you that Kent told all his relatives that he wasn't going to go back to prison—that he would kill anybody who tried to stop him, and that included them if they said anything."

Ava nodded. "Are you worried about your own safety?"

Again, the two exchanged a long look. Margery spoke first. "We've lived a long time. We don't intend to die soon, but if we can save other people…" She shrugged.

"But you don't have to tell him we're the ones who came to you," Michael said. "He knows we don't have anything to do with the rest of that side of the family, so he probably wouldn't suspect us right off."

"We just thought you should know, in case you plan to go after him," Margery said. "People say things like that in movies and books, but I think Kent really means it."

"I knew there was something not right about him the first time I laid eyes on him," Michael said. "But nobody else would hear a word against him. They were all shocked when he shot all those people, but I wasn't."

"Is Kent armed?" Brady spoke up for the first time.

Michael swiveled to look back at him. "His cousin Jeff told me he had a Ruger 45 automatic pistol and a Beretta APX. And plenty of ammo."

"Mr. and Mrs. Blake, would you be willing to testify in court if Kent is apprehended?" Ava asked.

Michael Blake took his wife's hand. "Margery and I talked about this before we came here and we agreed we would testify if we had to. It's the right thing to do."

Ava nodded. "Thank you for coming forward," she said. "We appreciate it. Is there anything else?"

"That's it." Michael pushed back from the table. "Except we'd like it if we could go out the back way. We don't want anyone to see us leaving here."

"Of course," she said.

"I'll see them out," Brady said.

He left and Ava sat at the table, digesting what the Blakes had just told her. It wasn't news that Kent Anderson had long declared he would kill any law enforcement officers who crossed his path, but according to Margery and Michael, he had expanded that threat to anyone—which could include an off-duty cop and a lost former DJ from Chicago.

Brady returned to the room. "We have to get word to Dillon," he said, as soon as the door was closed behind him.

Ava looked toward the recording equipment. "I shut it off before I left," Brady said. He sat across from her, in the chair recently vacated by Michael. "One of us needs to hike out there and find Dillon and Roslyn."

"I tried to get the chief to let me do it," Ava said. "He said he couldn't spare anyone. Without Dillon we're already shorthanded."

Brady pulled out his phone and began scrolling. "Dillon hasn't answered any of my texts. There's a lot of places out there with no cell coverage."

"I heard the fire burned a cell tower, which could make things worse." She drummed her pen on the table, trying to think what to do. "We should talk to the chief again. With this new information he might see things our way."

"Let me check with Search and Rescue first," Brady said. "Maybe they know more about what's going on with Dillon and Roslyn." He punched a number into the phone and put the call on speaker while it rang.

"Hello, Brady." Mountaintop Search and Rescue Commander Andrea Wayne's voice sounded clearly in the still room.

"Hey, Andrea," Brady said. "Have you heard anything from Dillon?"

"No. And one of our repeaters is down, so we can't raise him on the radio." The repeater system that relayed emergency signals to more remote parts of the county was subject to the whims of weather.

"I had a message yesterday that he and Roslyn Kern planned to spend the night at the caves above Cow Creek," Brady said. "But if they did that, they should have hiked out by now."

"Depends on how badly injured Ms. Kern is," Andrea said. "They may be taking it slower because of that, and because of her pregnancy."

"Then she really is pregnant?" Brady asked. "That isn't just speculation from news media?"

"The friends who reported her missing confirmed that she's about five months along. Maybe one of them said something to the press."

"Ava and I were thinking of hiking out to meet them," Brady said.

"We're already on it," Andrea said. "I've got a team ready to head up the trail with a litter and first aid supplies. We're leaving for the trailhead now."

Ava shook her head vigorously. "Don't do that," Brady said. "It's too dangerous."

"The fire isn't anywhere near the trail now," Andrea said. "There's a little smoke, but there's no immediate danger."

"The fire may not be near there, but we have reason to believe Kent Anderson is," Brady said. "And you didn't hear that from me. But Anderson is armed and dangerous. He may not readily distinguish between uniformed search and rescue volunteers and uniformed law enforcement. And he's sworn to kill law enforcement."

"Does Dillon know about this?"

"No. That's another reason Ava and I intend to head out there."

"Roslyn Kern may need help getting out of there."

"Your people can stage at the trailhead and we'll call if we need them," Brady said. "But don't head out on your own. Give us time to get there first."

"Don't worry. We don't take unnecessary risks."

"I'll be in touch," Brady said. "For now, sit tight." He ended the call. "Let's go talk to the chief."

CHIEF WALTERS WAS at his desk when Captain Rutledge stepped in. "Diaz has done it this time," he said.

Walters regarded Rutledge calmly. He had learned long ago that his definition of something worth getting upset about and the captain's were very different. "Is Diaz back?" he asked. "Is Roslyn Kern all right?"

"No, he's not back. But when he gets back, he's in for it. Take a look at this." Rutledge dropped a printout onto Walters's desk. "That's a screenshot from the *Tattler* website."

"Since when do you read the *Tattler*—whatever that is?" Walters asked.

Rutledge's face turned a darker shade of red. "Since a search of Roslyn Kern's name brings this up as one of the most-viewed sites related to her."

"Why are you searching for Ms. Kern's name on a website?" Walters asked. "As far as we're aware, she hasn't broken any laws."

"As public information officer, it's my job to keep up with what people are saying about our department."

"But you weren't searching our department name. Or were you?"

"The press is roasting us for not having rescued Ms. Kern yet."

"There are always going to be people who criticize the way we do our jobs, Arthur," Walters said. "It doesn't matter what some website named the

Tattler says. Nobody pays attention to that kind of thing."

Rutledge tapped the desk. "Read the printout."

Walters looked down at the paper and read out loud. "The hunky cop who raced to the rescue of Rockin' Roz Kern." This headline was followed by a picture of Dillon and his search dog, Bentley, from a fundraising calendar Search and Rescue had printed up last year. Dillon, in a muscle shirt and hiking pants, was flexing his biceps and grinning at the camera. Walters chuckled. "I guess they know what sells ads, or pulls in views, or however these sites make their money."

"Read the article," Rutledge said through clenched teeth.

Walters read, "Meet the man who is facing down wildfire and an escaped killer to bring radio sweetheart Roslyn 'Rockin' Roz' Kern to safety in the Idaho wilderness. Jasper Police Sergeant and local heartthrob Dillon Diaz loves dogs and kids and the ladies love him." Below this were photos of Dillon and Roslyn side by side, surrounded by heart emojis. Walters laughed. "Dillon is never going to live this down," he said.

"It makes us look like a bunch of lightweights," Rutledge said. "Playboys."

"Are you jealous, Arthur?" Rutledge was single, too, and bragged about his prowess with women. Seeing the twenty-years-younger Dillon lauded in the press probably got to him.

"I'm not jealous, I'm appalled. You never should

have allowed him to pose for that cheesy calendar. And working for Search and Rescue is a conflict of interest."

"I don't see it that way," Walters said. "As for the calendar, it was for a good cause, and I don't control what my officers do on their own time, as long as it's not illegal, of course." He crumpled up the print-out and tossed it into the trash can beside his desk. "Have we had any word from Dillon?"

"No," Rutledge said. "And I don't understand what's taking him so long. All he had to do was hike out of there on a marked trail."

"My understanding is Ms. Kern is pregnant and injured."

"Then why didn't he ask for more help when he still had a phone and radio signal?"

"Maybe we should send a couple of officers to look for them after all," Walters said. He had expected Dillon back by now. The fact that he wasn't pointed to trouble.

"You said it yourself. We don't have the manpower for that," Rutledge said. "We need every available body out there patrolling, with the town as packed as it is."

"Does that include you?"

"I'm too busy dealing with the press." Rutledge waved his hand toward the front of the building. "Have you seen the crowd of reporters out there? They're clamoring for information. I really think we should hold a press conference."

"To tell them what?" Walters asked. "We don't

have an update on Roslyn Kern, and I'm not giving them any information about Kent Anderson." Not that they had much to go on about the fugitive, but the press would be sure to ask. They had latched on to the idea that Anderson intended to harm Roslyn and were running with it. "I'm not going to feed the media anything else they can blow out of proportion."

"You don't have to participate," Rutledge said. "I could reassure them we're doing everything in our power to rescue Ms. Kern and we're keeping a close eye on the situation."

Ah. Walters saw what was going on now. Rutledge wanted an excuse to preen before the cameras. "No," he said. "No press conference. Not until we have something to report."

A knock on the door made them turn. "Come in," Walters called.

Ava entered the room, followed by Brady. The small office was getting more crowded by the second. "Sir, we have some new information about Kent Anderson," Ava said.

"What new information?" Rutledge demanded. "Why haven't I heard about this?"

Ava didn't roll her eyes at him, but Walters could read the desire to do so clearly written on her face. "What do you have?" he asked.

"A couple came into the station a little earlier, wanting to speak to an officer," Ava said. "I took them into an interview room and talked to them. Turns out they're two of Kent Anderson's relatives who live here in Jasper. Margery and Michael Blake. I asked Brady to sit in on the interview with me."

"Why did you interview these people?" Rutledge asked. "You should have passed them to me or to the chief."

"You weren't here and the chief was on the phone," Ava said. She looked back to Walters. "The Blakes say they only just found out that some of Anderson's other relatives helped him to escape. He says they were bragging about it."

"Who did they say was helping Anderson?" Walters asked.

"They gave us the names of several relatives who claim to have abetted Anderson," Brady said. "And they said they weren't aware that Donald Aldeen and Kent Anderson were friends, and they were sure Kent was headed to Alaska, not Nevada. The Blakes were very cooperative and willing to testify."

Walters nodded. "Do you have signed statements from both of them?"

"Yes, sir," Ava said. "But that's not all they told us. They said Anderson is definitely armed—two automatic pistols, a Ruger 45 automatic pistol and a Beretta APX."

"And plenty of ammunition," Brady added.

"They also said Anderson swore he wouldn't be taken back to jail alive," Ava said. "He intends to kill anyone who comes after him."

"He's sworn before to kill law enforcement officers," Brady said. "But this sounds like he'll shoot anyone he thinks is in his way. That could include

Dillon and Ms. Kern, if he comes across them on the trail."

"I really think we need to send officers to warn and help Dillon," Ava said. "Brady and I are volunteering to go. And Lacey."

"I spoke with Andrea Wayne of Mountaintop SAR and she hasn't heard anything from Dillon," Brady said. "She was getting a team ready to go looking for them, but I persuaded her to wait until she heard back from us."

"We're afraid Anderson might see the SAR uniforms and mistake the rescue volunteers for cops," Ava said.

"Where are the Blakes now?" Rutledge asked. "Did you detain them?"

"They came in voluntarily and told us what they knew," Ava said. "We had no reason to detain them."

"They may know more they didn't tell you," Rutledge said. "Or they were setting us up for a trap."

"Shut up, Arthur." Walters focused his attention on his officers. "They were sure about the weapons?" he asked.

"Yes, sir," Ava said. "They were very definite."

"If I send you two out there, Anderson will make you as cops before you ever see him," Walters said.

"Not if we're not in uniform," Brady said. "We figured we'll just be a couple out for a walk with their dog."

"On a trail that's closed because of fire danger?" Rutledge scoffed.

"Anderson has been in the wilderness since before

the trail was closed," Brady said. "Even if he knows the trail was shut down, we could just as easily have opened it up again now that the fire is moving away."

"If Anderson's goal is to escape, I doubt he'd be moving back toward town," Walters said.

"Unless he's following Dillon and Roslyn," Ava said. "That report from Kaitlyn Elwood about seeing a man who fit Anderson's description on her property this morning puts him a lot closer to Dillon and Roslyn than he should be if he's heading toward Alaska."

Walters considered this. He didn't like putting more officers at risk, but going in with SWAT or a bigger team would alarm Anderson and likely backfire. In the best-case scenario, Ava and Brady would find Dillon and Roslyn and help them get back to the trail safely. If not…he would have to trust his officers to be careful. "If you spot Anderson, don't approach him if you can avoid doing so," he said. "Call for backup, even if that means hiking back to the trailhead to do so. Don't take unnecessary risks."

"Yes, sir," Ava said.

"We'll be careful," Brady said.

"Then you can go," Walters said. "I want regular updates on your position."

"Yes, sir," Ava said. "Thank you."

"There's one more problem," Rutledge said.

They all turned toward him. "I've had word that there's a group of media at the Williams Gap Trailhead," Rutledge said. "They're anticipating Dillon and Roslyn Kern showing up there."

"How do we know some of them haven't already started down the trail?" Brady asked.

"I put one of our reserve officers—Castleberg— there to enforce the trail closure," Rutledge said. "I checked with him less than half an hour ago and he says so far everyone is being compliant."

"So we'll need to sneak past the media to get onto the trail," Brady said.

"We can start from the Elwoods' house," Ava said. "Kaitlyn said her property backs up to the trail."

"Do that," Walters agreed. "Now go change and get going."

They left the office. "Do you really think that was a good idea?" Rutledge asked.

"If I didn't send them and Dillon ended up having to face off against Anderson alone, they'd never forgive themselves," Walters said. He'd carry that guilt with him, too, added to the burden of all the regrets he'd accumulated during a long command. You couldn't always do the right thing in every situation. But he considered it a point of honor to keep trying. Once he stopped trying, it truly would be time to hang up his badge.

"There's still the problem of the media gathered at the trailhead," Rutledge said. "One reserve officer probably isn't going to be able to stop someone who's determined to head down the trail to meet Roslyn and Dillon and get the scoop."

"We don't have the personnel to put more officers on the scene," Walters said. "Unless you're suggesting you go."

"I've got a better idea," Rutledge said.

"What is that?"

"Let me hold a press conference here. I'll send word to the reporters at the trailhead that we have big news. None of them will want to miss that."

"And what big news do you plan to share with them?"

Rutledge waved his hand. "I'll think of something to get their attention, without revealing anything critical to the search for Anderson."

He probably would, too. Say what you would about Arthur, but he had a knack for giving the media what they wanted. "All right," Walters said. "But get busy. We don't have time to waste."

Chapter Fourteen

Roslyn remembered a time not that many months ago, when walking three miles would have been no challenge to her, but these last three miles to Jasper were taking forever. She was reduced to hobbling along on her swollen ankle, doing anything she could to distract herself from the discomfort. Dillon kept her going, encouraging her, waiting for her and urging her to rest. And thinking about him was a good way to avoid focusing on the pain. Dillon as he was now, and Dillon as he had been when they had met on Brundage Mountain.

"I've never been to McCall," she'd told him as they strolled down the town's main street the Sunday after Valentine's Day. They had forsaken the slopes for sightseeing, with Dillon eager to show her a place he knew well.

"What made you decide to come to Brundage?" he'd asked. "It's not exactly well-known."

"I was looking for someplace smaller and off the beaten path." She'd glanced at him. He was so gorgeous, giving off a lumberjack vibe that day in a buffalo plaid jacket and a sheepskin-lined cap with ear flaps.

"I get it," he said. "Hiding from the paparazzi." He laughed at what he had probably meant as a joke, but he didn't know how close to the truth he was.

"Something like that," she said. She hooked her arm in his. "Like I said, it's a really cute town." They passed a candy store, the front window filled with displays of truffles, decorated gingerbread and candy apples.

"You should come back in the summer," he said. "There's boating and swimming on Paiute Lake and a great beach area. And there's tons of hiking. I'd love to show it to you."

Her first impulse had been to declare that yes, she would love to come back and spend more time with him, but she'd pushed that away. That weekend hadn't been about building a relationship for the future. It was about nurturing the fantasy of now. It was an interval of passion, between two people who would never argue over whose turn it was to do the dishes, or who was going to call and deal with the apartment super. And she was a woman of mystery enjoying an assignation with a sexy lover. So she'd only smiled enigmatically and said, "Maybe I'll see it one day."

And now one day had come, and not only was she no longer a sexy woman of mystery, but she was a limping, pregnant female who hadn't had the sense to stay with her hiking group, necessitating a search and rescue mission. Dillon was seeing her with messy hair and no makeup, and right this minute she couldn't think of a time when she had felt less sexy.

He looked back at her now and smiled. "How are you doing?"

"I'm hanging in there." She tried to stand up straighter and not think about how her back was aching almost as badly as her ankle. "Have you ever done anything like this before?"

"Like what?"

"Have to hike out of the wilderness with someone you've rescued?"

"No," he said. "Usually there's a whole team working a rescue. If not for the fire cutting off the trail, we would have carried you out on a litter, and you would have probably been back at your rooms by nightfall."

And he would have been in his house—the house he bought for a family he didn't yet have. "If you hadn't been stuck with me for the last twenty-four hours, what do you think would have happened?" she asked. "When you found out about the baby, what would you have done?"

He considered the question for a long moment. She listened to her heart pounding, knowing how much the answer meant to her. "I would have stayed with you," he said. "I would have tried to figure out what you wanted from me, and how I could help with the baby."

"I didn't come here looking for money." The thought horrified her. Though legally he might be obligated to support her, she was making a good living and didn't want him to think this was all about finances. "I just thought you'd want to know."

"I'll support my child," he said, a little stiffly. "And I'll try to be a good father." His expression softened a little. "And I want us to be good friends, too. However we end up handling the parenting."

"It's terrifying sometimes, thinking of being responsible for a life," she said. "What if we mess things up?"

"I think you'll be a wonderful mom," he said.

She was mortified to find she was crying, but she couldn't stop herself. She hadn't even realized until now how much she had longed for someone to say that—to reassure her that at some point instinct would take over and she would know how to care for this child. That it would be him—the one person who would have the most right to question her decisions and choices—undid her.

She stood in the middle of the path, blubbering, until he came and gathered her into his arms. "You're tired and hurting, and probably hungry and thirsty, too," he said. "But you're doing great. This will all be over soon. Just a little farther."

"Are you going to tell me that when I'm in labor, too?" She blushed as soon as she said the words, but the image of him by her side while she brought their child into the world was a powerful one. He had been her rock through this ordeal, so why not depend on him for an even greater trial?

"If you want me to, I will," he said, with all the solemnity of an oath.

She closed her eyes and rested her head on his chest, listening to the steady beat of his heart, feeling the strength in his arms as he held her. All these months she had been telling herself she was strong enough to carry this baby alone. She was strong enough to give birth alone and to raise a child by herself.

But she didn't have to be that strong now. Dillon wanted to share the burden, and finally, standing here in the middle of nowhere, as worn down as she had ever been, she was ready to believe him.

She didn't know what kind of future they would have together, but right now, she would hold on to the promise that he would be there for her and for their child. It was far more than she had ever expected.

DILLON WALKED SLOWER and slower, but still Roslyn struggled to keep up. She had recovered her spirits somewhat but was still limping badly, and she stopped frequently to arch her back and knead at her spine, her brow furrowed in pain. "Is something wrong?" he asked, alarmed.

She shook her head. "The baby is fine," she said. "And I'm fine. I promise." She started walking again, doing her best to increase her pace, but he could see what the effort cost her.

"Let's stop and rest," he said.

"We just stopped not long ago."

Yes, when she had been crying, as if something

he said had upset her. She seemed so fragile right now he was hesitant to say anything, but more rest was something he could be sure about. "We can stop again," he said. "We've got hours of daylight left."

She nodded. "All right. But I feel terrible that I'm going so slowly. You would have been out of here hours ago if it wasn't for me."

It was true they were moving at a crawl. He estimated they had come barely half a mile in the last hour. "I'm not going anywhere without you," he said. He moved in beside her and put his arm around her waist, supporting some of her weight. He searched for somewhere comfortable to sit, but there was really nowhere in this open area. He guided her to the side of the trail and lowered her to a patch of grass. "Let's see your ankle again."

He unlaced her boot and drew it off, aware of her wincing as he did so. "It's more swollen, isn't it?" she asked, leaning over to look as he peeled off her sock.

He nodded. The standard treatment for a sprain was rest, ice, compression and gentle exercise. Roslyn was getting none of that right now and her ankle was protesting. "Let's see if a cool compress helps," he said. He took out a water bottle and a square of gauze and applied the damp gauze around the ankle. "We'll leave that there for a while." Then he took out his phone.

"Any signal?" she asked.

"No." He stared at the No Service message on his screen. His radio also produced nothing but static.

He wanted to get in touch with Search and Rescue and ask them to send a team with a litter for Roslyn.

"Guess we're going to have to tough it out and keep going," she said.

He liked her attitude, but he hated seeing her in pain. "Maybe I could carry you," he said.

She snorted. "Please! You'd ruin your back. Or you'd trip and drop me."

"Hey, I'm not that clumsy."

Her smile was so tender it moved him. "You're not," she said. "You've been great."

He touched a finger to the side of her mouth. "I was attracted to you from the very first by this smile. It stopped me cold in that lift line and I told myself I had to meet a woman with a smile like that."

"And we ended up on the chair together," she said.

"Oh, I made sure that happened," he said. "I let the couple in front of me go ahead so you and I would be sure to match up."

She laughed. "I was watching you and wondered."

"So you noticed me, too?" he asked.

"Oh, yeah. I thought you were hot."

He laughed, a big, joyous laugh. "And then we got on the lift together and started talking and you were so charming," she said. "And funny. You made me laugh and I hadn't laughed in so long."

Some of the mirth went out of him. "I'm sorry you had to go through so much heartache," he said. She hadn't said much at the time, only that she had recently broken up with someone. They hadn't been into talking about their histories or the future, only focused on the present.

"Thanks." She brushed her hair back from her eyes. "It didn't feel like it at the time, but I can see how much better off I am now."

"That's good. You seem happy."

"I have a lot to be happy about." She smiled down at her baby bump.

He settled in to sit beside her. Columns of smoke were visible in the distance, but directly overhead the sky was deep blue, and everything was peaceful. "Do you think you'll stay in Chicago?" he asked. When she had said earlier that she could work anywhere, he had hoped she was hinting that she might want to move closer to him.

"I don't know," she said. "I have friends there, and a nice apartment, but there's nothing to really anchor me there. We moved around a lot when I was a kid, so no one place has ever felt like home." She glanced at him. "Not like you."

"You already know I love it here, but I think you'd like it here, too."

"Why do you think that?" She was genuinely curious. Did he see something in her that she didn't?

"You like photography, right?"

She nodded.

"The scenery here draws photographers from around the world. In every season of the year there's natural beauty to capture with a camera. And you like the outdoors, at least judging by your hiking boots. You've put a few miles on those."

"I do enjoy hiking," she said.

"And skiing," he added. "You're a lot closer to Brundage Mountain here than you are in Chicago, not to mention Jackson Hole."

"I've always wanted to ski Jackson," she said.

"And there's peace and quiet. You need that for recording, right? There's plenty of peace and quiet here." Was he pouring it on too thick?

She laughed. "You're doing your best to convince me."

"I'm not trying to pressure you," he said. "But I could be a lot more help to you and the baby if you were closer."

"I'll seriously consider it," she said. "And it would be good for the baby to have his or her father close by." She frowned, a momentary wrinkling of her brow.

"What's wrong?" he asked.

She shook her head. "Nothing, really. It's just... your job. Isn't it dangerous?"

She really was giving this serious thought. He told himself that was a good sign. "It can be," he said. "But there's less crime here than in a city like Chicago. Probably because there are fewer people. There's still danger, but it's not a constant. We have some officers who come from a big city environment and they all agree working in Jasper is a lot less stressful."

"I've never lived in a town so small," she said. "But I can see how it could be nice. Especially with a family. What brought your parents here?"

"Like I said, they moved from Denver. My dad had been fishing in the area and fell in love, and my mom wanted a bigger place. The two of them are usually on the same page about decisions like that."

"That's a good thing for a marriage."

"It is. It's funny, though—they only knew each other six weeks when they got married."

"You're kidding."

"I'm not." He shook his head. "I asked them about it and my dad said he fell hard for her right away and didn't want to waste any more time. My mom said she just knew Dad was the man she needed to spend the rest of her life with." He thought about how hard he had fallen for Roslyn, from that very first day in the lift line. He risked looking at her. Her eyes were misty.

"That's so romantic," she said.

Their eyes met and he felt again the pull of desire, of needing to be closer to her. He reached for her and she leaned toward him. Their lips met, and the emotion of the moment overwhelmed him—tenderness, protectiveness, longing, fear that what he felt was too fragile to last. The sensation was unsettling. He had never hesitated when it came to relationships. He went after what he wanted, and the women he had been with had all reciprocated his feelings, brief though they might have been at times.

But no woman had mattered to him the way Roslyn did. Was this what his dad had felt for his mom—this sensation that life without Roslyn in it would be a little dimmer, a little less complete?

She broke the kiss, her eyes looking deep into his, as if trying to read his thoughts. "Dillon, I—"

"Arf! Arf! Arf!" At their feet, Bentley erupted into fierce barking. He ran forward, leash trailing, the hair of his ruff standing on end, his whole body tense.

Dillon tensed also. He gently pushed Roslyn away from him and stood. "What is it, boy?" he asked, following the dog's gaze to the border of woodland to their far left. Had something moved within the shadows there?

"Arf! Arf! Arf!" Bentley took off running toward the dim figure, Dillon right behind him.

EMMA HAD ONLY come downtown for a few minutes to pick up tidbits to entice some of the evacuees who were too upset to eat properly. She could have sent Barbara or one of her other helpers, but she thought it would be a good idea to take a break from the chaos at DCA. Barking dogs didn't really bother her after so long, but add in a steady stream of people looking to drop off or retrieve pets and it got to be a little much.

She was on her way back to her car when she noticed a crowd gathering near the police station. "What's going on?" she asked a well-dressed man who was walking briskly in that direction.

"The local police have called a press conference to release information about the hunt for Kent Anderson," the man said.

Emma followed him toward what turned out to

be a portable stage that looked suspiciously like the one the parks department used for summer concerts in the park. Directly in front of the police department, East Main had been closed off with barricades. Emma spotted Tashya's fiancé, Jason, at one of the barricades. "What's happening?" she asked, hoping for more specifics.

"Captain Rutledge is holding a press conference," Jason said. He stood straight and tall in his uniform and tried to look stern, but couldn't hold the expression when he asked, "Is Tashya with you?"

"Sorry, just me." Emma held up the bag from the local pet boutique, Chow. "I had to run a few errands. Why is Rutledge holding the conference instead of Chief Walters?"

Jason shrugged.

"Probably because the chief has better ways to spend his time than put on a show for the media." Emma leaned past Jason and squinted at Rutledge, who had just stepped onto the stage, sharp in dress blues, his hair carefully gelled. "Is he wearing makeup?"

Jason turned to look and his eyes widened. "I'm not sure he normally has that much color in his cheeks. Or his lips."

"I guess he figures if it's good enough for actors, it's good enough for him," Emma said.

A squawk from the sound system made her wince. Rutledge cleared his throat. "All right, everyone. Let's get started," he said.

The assembled media shifted and murmured. Rutledge cleared his throat again, consulted his notes, then began. "I'm Captain Arthur Rutledge with the Jasper Police Department. I know you have a lot of questions about the hunt for convicted mass murderer Kent Anderson, as well as the search for Roslyn Kern, but I want to assure you we have the situation in hand and expect to have Anderson back in custody and Ms. Kern restored to safety within a matter of hours."

"We do?" murmured Jason.

No one but Emma heard him in the uproar that followed these claims. "Does this mean you know Anderson's whereabouts?" someone called.

"Are the federal authorities who are leading the manhunt aware of this information?" someone else asked. "I thought they were looked for Anderson in Nevada."

"What about Ms. Kern?" a woman called. "Do you know where she is? Is she all right?"

"When will you be bringing Anderson into custody?"

"Are Roslyn Kern and Kent Anderson together?"

"How were you able to locate the two of them?"

Rutledge held up both hands, gesturing for calm. "We have one of our best officers with Ms. Kern now, escorting her back to safety," he said.

"What about Anderson?" a man directly in front of the stage asked.

"We are closing in on him," Rutledge said. "We have been tracking his progress for some time now 'and it's only a matter of time before we have him in custody."

Emma felt Jason tense beside her, but he said nothing.

"What about the federal marshals who are pursuing Anderson?" a woman Emma recognized as a news reporter from a Boise television station asked.

Rutledge scowled. "Anderson is in our jurisdiction," he said. "Jasper PD is better equipped to apprehend a fugitive here than people who are unfamiliar with the area."

"Did he just say we're better equipped than the Feds?" Jason whispered to Emma.

"That's what it sounded like to me," Emma said. The media would no doubt take that statement and run with it. Chief Walters would stroke out when he found out.

Rutledge ignored other questions fired his way, and droned on for several minutes about his experience with the department and plans for the future. "You're going to see a whole new era of policing in Jasper soon," he said.

"Are you saying Chief Walters intends to take the department in a new direction?" The reporter for the local paper, Pam Xavier, asked this question.

"Chief Walters will be retiring soon and his successor will focus on updating the department with the latest policing methods," Rutledge said.

"Who is Chief Walters's successor?" a woman asked.

"There's nothing official yet, but as the most senior officer on the force, I'm the most logical candidate for the position." Rutledge struck a pose as cameras flashed—chin up, steely glint in his eyes, Hollywood's perfect portrayal of a dedicated law enforcement officer.

"If he's made chief, the first thing he'll do is get rid of the canine program," Emma said. She kept her voice low but could barely contain her rage. She hoped her proposed training would help the captain deal with dogs in a less confrontational manner, but she had little faith she could turn him into a dog lover, or make him see the worth of Chief Walters's efforts to pair dogs and officers as a vital part of the public safety community here in Jasper.

"A lot of the officers won't like that." Jason looked at her, sadness in his eyes. "I was hoping to work with my own dog one day soon. Tashya and I had talked about it. When I'm ready."

"You'll do great with a dog," Emma said and squeezed his arm.

"That's all the questions we have time for," Rutledge said. "Thank you for coming."

"Wait! You haven't told us how you tracked down Anderson."

"When will Ms. Kern be returning to Jasper? Is she all right?"

"What were Anderson's intentions when he escaped? Why did he come to Jasper?"

Rutledge ignored the questions and turned away.

"Wait! I have something to say!"

Rutledge's eyes widened and he held up one hand,

as if trying to stop traffic, as a woman climbed the steps onto the stage. Colleen Diaz, her red hair caught up in a rhinestone clasp and her sapphire blue wrap dress accentuating a mature but curvaceous figure, strode to the microphone as if she was accustomed to addressing a crowd. "My name is Colleen Diaz and my son, Dillon, is the officer who is rescuing poor Ms. Kern," she announced.

Cameras flashed and a new energy surged through the crowd of media. "I hope they run those photos on a lot of front pages," Emma said, smiling. "Rutledge might burst into flames with envy."

Jason chuckled but quickly resumed a straight face.

"Have you spoken with your son today?" someone asked. "Is Roslyn all right?"

"How did he find her?"

"Have they seen Kent Anderson? Has he threatened him?"

"Dillon is very good at his job," Colleen said. "So of course he was able to locate Ms. Kern. I haven't spoken to him this morning, but this young woman, Roslyn Kern, is in very good hands now. Dillon is not only an excellent police officer and a wonderful son, he's also very good-looking."

Laughter rippled through the crowd. Colleen's smile broadened. "I know a mother is always biased, but you ladies out there have seen his photo and you know, right?"

More laughter. Someone else in this situation might have come across looking ridiculous, but Colleen was charming them all—a talent she had passed on to her oldest son.

"Is Dillon single?" someone asked.

"He is! And so is Ms. Kern." Colleen winked. "It's a very romantic scenario, don't you think? A young woman in need of assistance, and a handsome, dedicated young man in need of the right woman in his life."

"Are you saying your son and Roslyn Kern are romantically involved?"

Colleen gave an elegant shrug. "There are worse ways to begin a relationship."

Emma couldn't keep back her laughter. "Dillon is never going to hear the end of this," she said.

"Who knows?" Jason said. "She could be right."

"What?" Emma stared at him. "You think Dillon and this stranger from Chicago could really end up together?"

"They'll have had plenty of time to get to know each other by the time this is all over."

"How long did you date Tashya before you proposed?" Emma asked, though she already knew the answer.

He flushed. "Three years. But we were teenagers when we met. And I don't know—a few things Dillon has said make me think he's ready to settle down."

Was he? Emma wondered. Dillon had always struck her as the type who liked to play the field. He never had to work to attract women, so why commit to one? Though supposedly he had fallen pretty hard for someone he met while skiing this past winter. But she'd heard that hadn't worked out.

"That's all we have time for." Rutledge stepped in front of Colleen and took the microphone from its stand. "You can all leave now. This press conference is over."

Colleen leaned close to Rutledge to speak into the mic. "Thank you, Captain Rutledge," she said. "It was so nice to hear you acknowledge my son as one of your best officers. It makes me so proud."

Faced with the full force of both Colleen's personality and her physical presence, Rutledge could only looked stunned. Only when she had sashayed away did he find his voice once more. "What are you doing just standing there?" he barked at Jason. "Get that street reopened, then return to patrol."

"Yes, sir." Jason hefted one of the barricades.

"I'll leave you to it," Emma said. She smiled and waved at the scowling Rutledge and headed back toward her car. He seemed confident that he would soon be in charge of Jasper PD, but she wasn't so sure about that. Not if his plans meant getting rid of the dogs.

Chapter Fifteen

Ava and Brady, with Lacey between them, drove slowly past the Williams Gap Trailhead. Search and Rescue was there, with an ambulance and the Jeep used to transport personnel. Andrea and several other SAR members stood around the back of the ambulance, all wearing bright yellow search and rescue vests. The yellow caution tape that had previously blocked the entrance fluttered loosely from one of the posts marking the entrance. A couple of cars with Idaho plates sat on the far side of the parking area. The bright yellow warning sign Ava had posted yesterday was still in place at the entrance to the trail.

"Those two on the edge are rental cars," Brady said as he eased his truck past. "Probably reporters."

"I see two people standing by the trail map, talking," Ava said. "That's probably them."

"Everyone else must have taken Captain Rutledge's bait and gone to the press conference," Brady said.

"What should we do?" Ava asked. "If we park at

the trailhead, they'll have questions, and they might make us for cops."

"We can head to the Elwoods' house and cut across from there to the trail," Brady said. "But I'm afraid if we do that, we'll miss Dillon and Roz. We don't know how fast they're traveling, and it's possible they're closer to the trail's end by now."

Ava nodded. "So, do you have a plan C?"

"We could park down the road," he said. "There's a gate to a hayfield. There's a path that runs from there and hits the trail a few hundred yards past the start."

They left the truck at the gate, climbed over a stile and followed a faint trail through tall grass to the more defined trail. "This leads up to Cow Creek," Brady said, checking the GPS on his phone. "This should be the path Dillon and Roslyn take."

The plan was for them to hike until they met Dillon, keeping an eye out for Kent Anderson or any sign of trouble. They set out with Lacey in the lead, loping along at a steady, brisk pace. "I'm a little freaked out, crossing this open section," Ava said. "What if Anderson is watching us?"

"What if he's not out here at all?" Brady said. He scanned their surroundings—tall grass beginning to yellow at the tips, and stands of dark evergreens and lighter aspen to their left. Not a single wisp of cloud marred the perfect blue of the sky, and the only sounds were their footsteps crunching on the trail and the jingle of Lacey's tags.

"It's too quiet," Ava said. "Where are the birds?"

"I thought you were a city girl," Brady said.

"I've been doing a lot of hiking lately," she said. "With Eli and by myself. I've discovered I like the outdoors."

"Next thing you know, we'll have you rafting rivers and climbing cliffs," Brady said.

"I'd like to do those things and more," she said. "And I'd do them better than you."

"You could try," he said.

"Shh!" She held up a hand to silence him and nodded toward the dog. Lacey stood frozen in the middle of the trail, tail low, ears forward, staring intently into the trees.

"Can you tell what she's alerting on?" Brady asked. He slid his Glock from its holster and held it loose at his side.

Ava shook her head. The three of them stood there for a long moment, the two people watching the dog. Brady tried to slow his breathing, eyes straining into the woods, trying to see what the dog saw. Or smelled. Or felt with that sixth sense some dogs seemed to have.

"Lacey, seek!" Ava commanded.

The dog glanced back at her.

"Seek!" Ava said again.

Lacey trotted off the trail and into the woods, the two humans jogging to keep up.

HEART POUNDING, ROSLYN stared as Dillon headed after Bentley. "What is it?" she called. "Why is he barking like that?" This was definitely a different sound than when Bentley had alerted them to the presence of the deer earlier.

"I don't know," Dillon called back. "But stay here."

She glanced down at her bare foot, the ankle still wrapped in wet gauze. It wasn't as if she could go anywhere like this. But just in case, she decided she'd better put her sock and boot back on.

She finished lacing up her boot and stood, trying out the ankle. It still hurt, but she was determined to keep going. They were so close to safety and rest. She had never wanted a hot shower so much in her life. And after that…after that, she and Dillon needed to have a serious talk about the future. She had to tell him she wanted them to be more than two people with only a child in common. She would never have believed she could have such intense feelings for a man she had known for only a short time, but she wanted the chance to nurture those feelings.

When he had talked about his home, and his desire to raise a family there, it had been all she could do not to shout, *I want to be part of that family, too. I want that to be us in that house, raising our child together.*

She glanced toward the woods, where Dillon and Bentley had disappeared among the trees. She felt shaky—and afraid. Had the man who had tried to steal her camera returned? Would Bentley frighten him away? Or would he hurt the dog—or hurt Dillon? She put a hand over her heart, trying to quell the fear that welled inside her.

"Stand right there and don't move."

The man's voice was deep and hoarse, and she let out a squeak of surprise at his words and started to turn around.

"I told you not to move!" he shouted.

She froze, and clenched her jaw to keep from crying out again.

"Where's the camera?" he asked.

"The camera?"

"You were taking pictures. You had a camera."

This was the man who had tried to steal her camera earlier! The knowledge made her shake. She took a deep breath. *Stay strong,* she told herself. *Your only chance is to be smarter than he is.* And hope that Dillon returned soon. "It's in my pack." She gestured toward the pack, which rested on the ground.

"Get it and toss it over here," he said. "The whole pack."

Moving slowly, she sidestepped toward the pack, imagining the man pointing a gun at her. But she didn't know that, did she? What if he was bluffing? She reached the pack and bent to pick it up by the straps, but as she did so, she looked back, and started shaking again.

Yes, he had a gun pointed at her. She didn't know anything about guns, but this looked like a big pistol. And he was close. Maybe ten feet from her. Even a little gun could probably kill her from that distance.

"Throw it over here!" he ordered.

She did as he asked, though her toss was weak. The pack landed halfway between them. If the man wanted it, he'd have to move closer. Which would bring the gun closer. "Why do you want my camera?" she asked. She didn't care about his answer, but she wanted to buy time for Dillon to return to her.

Then what? He was a cop. He was armed. And he had Bentley with him. But what if the man shot them? Maybe she should be doing everything she could to keep them from returning to her. "There's just a bunch of pictures of wildflowers on there," she said.

"I saw you aiming the camera at me," the man said. She had been so focused on the gun that she hadn't noticed much about him, but she had the impression of blandness—bland clothes and hair and very ordinary looks. Only the gun made him sinister, and the way he had it trained on her.

"Is that why you've been following us?" she asked. "Because you don't like your picture being taken?"

"Shut up. You ask too many questions."

She heard a shuffling sound in the grass, and sensed him moving toward her. She tensed, imagining the bullet striking her at any moment. But as she waited, movement ahead of her caught her eye. Dillon and Bentley appeared at the edge of the woods, moving toward her. *Stay back!* She wanted to shout to them. And *help me!*

She risked a look back, and the man moved closer to her. Maybe she could distract him so he wouldn't see Dillon.

"Turn back around!" he barked.

"Why should I?" she asked. "If I took your picture, I already know what you look like. And what does that matter anyway? Who are you?"

"You don't know who I am?" He had reached the backpack now. He picked it up and slung it over his shoulder.

"No." She squinted, as if trying to bring him into better focus. There was nothing remarkable about the man. "Are you famous?"

His laughter at this comment startled her. "Are you really as dumb as you sound?" he asked. "Or are you only pretending?"

She glared at him. "I might be ignorant, but I'm not stupid," she said.

"Stop right there! Don't move!"

Dillon's voice rang across the clearing. Roslyn turned toward him and her heart leaped to see him standing there, a pistol aimed at the man who had accosted her.

"You shoot me and I'll kill her," the man shouted. "This close, I won't miss." A sharp click of his weapon being cocked, and Roslyn forgot how to breathe.

Chapter Sixteen

Dillon froze, paralyzed by the sight of the gun trained on Roslyn. "Drop the gun!" Anderson ordered. Dillon opened his hand and let the gun fall. It seemed to take forever to hit the ground, time slowed down by the cold fear that gripped him. Beside him, Bentley quivered, a low growl rising from deep in the dog's chest. Dillon told himself he should signal the dog to stay, but he was unable to move. *Breathe*, he reminded himself, and did so. *Think*.

"Don't be a fool, Kent," he said.

"How do you know my name?"

"Every law officer in the state is looking for you," Dillon said. "There's a SWAT team on its way here right now."

"You're a liar," Anderson said. "But even if you aren't, I'll be gone before they get here. I'm not going back to prison. Never."

Dillon had seen images of Anderson on television right after he was captured. He had looked small and weak then, the kind of person whose only power is in the weapon they wield, not in their own character. Up close, he didn't look so small, but ordinary. If they had passed on the trail, Dillon would have taken him for just another hiker out enjoying the day.

"Get over here, by the woman." Anderson motioned with the gun. Moving to where Roslyn sat meant getting closer to Anderson, but not close enough to disarm him. One wrong move and Anderson would kill him. Then he'd be free to kill Roslyn, too. Dillon had to stay alive. As long as he was alive, they had a chance to get away, though he couldn't see a clear way to make that happen, yet.

He moved slowly, hands out at his sides in clear view. "Sit down next to her," Anderson ordered.

He sat, and Roslyn gave him a shaky smile. He looked into her eyes, trying to reassure her somehow, but she was clearly terrified, pupils wide, arms folded protectively across the swell of her abdomen. He focused on Anderson. The fugitive had turned to face them, holding the pistol in both hands, aimed at them. Dillon studied the gun—a 45, a Ruger, he thought, not that the make mattered. Anderson had plenty of firepower to kill them at this range.

Dillon kept his gaze fixed on Anderson but noticed out of the corner of his eye that Bentley hadn't followed him. Instead, the dog lay flat on his belly in the tall grass, scarcely visible except for the tips of his ears. Was the dog hiding because he was frightened?

"Why don't you just go and leave us alone?" Roslyn said. "It's not as if we can do anything to stop you."

"You'll tell the cops you saw me, and which direction I'm headed," Anderson said. "Right now, because of the fire, no one knows I'm out here. I'm going to make sure it stays that way."

"Law enforcement knows you're here," Dillon said.

Anderson glared at him. Dillon thought the fugitive was going to accuse him of lying again. Instead, Anderson took a step closer. "You're a cop, aren't you?" he asked, his face flushed. "I should have known. You look like a cop. You've been following me, haven't you?"

"No! He came out here to find me," Roslyn said. "I hurt my ankle and—"

"Shut up!" Anderson took better aim with the pistol. Dillon stared, bracing for the bullet's impact. He reached for Roslyn, wanting his last sensation to be of touching her.

He didn't see Bentley explode from his hiding place in the grass, but he saw the dog leap, his jaws latching on to Anderson's outstretched arm. Anderson shouted and flailed. Dillon jumped up as the gun went off, but the bullet didn't strike him. He rushed forward and grabbed Anderson's other arm and twisted it behind his back. Bentley held on to the other arm, even as Anderson struggled to free himself.

Dillon pulled Anderson to the ground and subdued him. "Bentley, leave it!" he ordered.

The dog released his hold and backed up, panting, gaze fixed on Dillon. Dillon pulled flex-cuffs from his pack and secured Anderson's hands behind his back. "Good boy," he told Bentley.

But the dog had already moved away, to Roslyn. The dog whined and pawed at the woman, who lay on her side, moaning. "Roslyn!" Dillon abandoned Anderson and raced to her side.

Roslyn stared up at him, her cheeks streaked with tears. "He shot me," she said.

"Where? Where did he shoot you?" Fighting panic, Dillon knelt beside her.

"My arm." She rolled onto her back and he saw blood welling from a wound in her biceps.

"It's going to be okay," he said, to himself as well as to her. "I'm going to stop the bleeding and we're going to get you to the hospital and everything is going to be okay." How he was going to do that, he had no clear idea, but if he had to carry her on his back all the way to town, he would do it.

AVA AND BRADY heard the gunshots and someone screaming. Lacey barked and launched herself toward the sound, leaping through the underbrush until Ava lost sight of her. Someone was shouting now, and another dog barking. Was that Bentley? Ava pushed herself to run harder, feet pounding on the leaf mold, ducking to dodge branches, her pack bouncing against her back. Her ballistics vest dug into her bottom rib, but she ignored the pain and pushed on. Who had screamed? Was that Anderson shooting? Or Dillon? Was someone hurt? Were they running to rescue, or into an ambush?

DILLON PULLED A stack of gauze pads from his pack and pressed them to Roslyn's shoulder. She cried out at the pressure. "I know it hurts," he said. "But we have to stop the bleeding." He looked around them, hoping to see help approaching. Anderson lay on the ground glaring at him. How long before he made a move to run, or to attack?

At first Dillon thought he might be hallucinating. A large, dark dog burst from the trees and raced toward them, followed by two running humans. Bentley barked, tail wagging, and Anderson let out a string of curses as the other dog skidded to a stop in front of the prisoner and sat. He recognized Ava's partner, Lacey.

Dillon raised one arm to wave. "Over here!" he shouted to the people, who had slowed and were looking around, weapons drawn. "We need help!"

"Who is it?" Roslyn asked. She lay with her back to the trail now, eyes closed, her breathing shallow.

"Ava Callan and Brady Nichols, with the Jasper Police," Dillon said, as the two raced toward them.

"What happened?" Ava looked from the prone figure of Anderson to the gentle mound of Roslyn's belly.

"This is Kent Anderson," Dillon said. "He shot Roslyn Kern." He looked down to where he still pressed gauze to Roslyn's arm. "She's lost some blood but she's going to be all right. But we need a litter team to carry her out, and an ambulance waiting at the trailhead."

"I'll run back for help," Ava said. "Lacey can stay

here and help with Anderson." The dog sat by Anderson's head, and let out a low rumble when the fugitive raised his head.

"Good idea," Brady said.

Ava took off running. Things happened quickly after that. Brady took charge of Anderson while Dillon finished bandaging Roslyn. "How did you know to come looking for us?" Dillon asked.

"We were pretty sure Anderson was in the area and worried you might cross paths," Brady said. "He had sworn to kill anyone who interfered with his escape." He relieved Anderson of another gun, a knife and his pack, ignoring the fugitive's cursing and complaining as he worked. He turned to Roslyn, who stared up at him. "I'm Brady Nichols, by the way," he said.

"Hello. I'm Roslyn Kern."

"Oh, we all know who you are," Brady said. He tagged and bagged Anderson's weapons as he spoke. "Jasper is full of media right now, all covering the story of Rockin' Roz lost in the wilderness."

Roslyn moaned and closed her eyes. "I can't believe they followed me here."

"I don't think they followed you," Brady said. "I think they were in town because of the fire, and because Kent Anderson escaped from prison. Apparently, he had relatives in the area who helped him get away and he planned to head to Alaska. But once you went missing, that was one more story to add to the news cycle." He turned to Dillon. "How did the two of you meet up with Anderson?"

"He's been following us since I found Roslyn." Dillon rested his hand on Roslyn's. "While she was photographing wildflowers, she inadvertently caught Anderson in one of her shots. He realized it and thought when she showed the photo around, law enforcement would know where he was and come after him."

"Law enforcement has known where he was practically from the beginning," Brady said. "The man who gave him a ride to near the trailhead identified him in a photo lineup."

Anderson started swearing. Lacey growled again and he fell silent. Brady looked at Roslyn again. She lay with her eyes closed, her breathing shallow. "How's she doing?"

"She's going to be okay." Dillon squeezed her hand.

"Just to warn you, there are a lot of reporters in town who are going to be excited to see her," Brady said. "We don't get celebrities in Jasper all that often."

"She's not just a celebrity," Dillon said. He smiled down at Roslyn. "Brady, meet Rosie Kenley, aka Roslyn Kern."

Brady stopped what he was doing and stared. "So you finally found Rosie," he said. He eyed the baby bump again. Dillon could almost see him doing the math in his head.

Roslyn, who had fallen quiet while they talked, opened her eyes and said, "Yes, the baby is Dillon's. Now could I have some water, please?"

Both men hurried to offer water, but Dillon won out. He held her head while she drank and watched blood seep through the bandage he had wrapped around her upper arm. How long was it going to take Ava to get to help, and how long after that for help to get to them?

"Search and Rescue is staged at the trailhead," Brady said. "Once they get the word, it won't take them long to get here."

"That's good," Dillon said.

"There's going to be a circus once word gets out you've been found," Brady said. "And Anderson. The media have really been playing up the idea of the beautiful DJ being pursued through the wilderness by a wildfire and an escaped killer. That is, those reporters who haven't decided that Roz and Kent are in this together." He pointed to Dillon. "And they've latched onto you as the hunky knight in shining armor who set out to rescue her."

"Welcome to my world," Roslyn said. Her eyes met Dillon's. "Sorry."

He squeezed her hand. "I can handle it."

"He thinks so," Brady said to Roslyn. "But wait until he sees the grief everyone back at the station is going to give him."

Bentley's barking interrupted the rude reply Dillon had in mind. Brady stood. "Looks like the cavalry is here," he said, and walked out to greet the EMTs and law enforcement headed toward them up the trail.

Dillon looked down at Roslyn. "How are you doing?" he asked.

"I'm hanging in there," she said. "How about you?"

"As long as you're good, I'm good." He laced his fingers with hers. "You're stuck with me now."

Her smile burned through him, like a brand on his heart. "I like the sound of that."

"You're doing great," Charla, the paramedic, said when she had finished checking Roslyn over. "The baby is doing fine, too."

Roslyn managed a smile. "That's good to know." She had been such a trouper through this whole ordeal—so brave and steady. She found Dillon and smiled a little wider at him. "Did you hear that? The baby is okay."

"I heard." He took her hand and held it all the way up the trail to the waiting ambulance. Though he saw Andrea and the other SAR members exchange questioning looks, no one said anything. Jason Wright and Cal Hoover arrived to take Kent Anderson into custody, and a crime scene team arrived to process the site of the shooting. Ava and Brady trailed Dillon and the SAR team to the ambulance, where Dillon finally released Roslyn's hand so she could be loaded into the ambulance.

"Do you want a ride to the hospital?" Brady asked as they watched the ambulance pull away, siren wailing.

Dillon shook his head. "Thanks, but Roslyn will

go straight into surgery and I'll drive myself crazy waiting for word from her. Better to go into the station and deal with all the paperwork."

"Then Anderson is all yours. You're the one who captured him. You deserve the glory."

"Right. You just don't want to deal with the press."

Brady clapped him on the back. "Hey, you're already a celebrity. Might as well run with it. And I guess congratulations are in order."

"Congratulations?" Ava asked. "For capturing Anderson?"

"Oh, you missed the big news," Brady said. He punched Dillon's arm—hard enough that he felt a sting, though he tried not to show it. "Dillon here is going to be a father."

"A father?" Ava looked confused, then her eyes widened. "You don't mean Roslyn Kern?"

"Roslyn is actually Rosie, the woman Dillon met over Valentine's weekend and has been searching for ever since."

Ava shook her head. "Okay. Well, congratulations!"

Dillon couldn't keep back a foolish grin. "Yeah. I'm still getting used to the idea."

They spent the ride to the station hearing a recap of Dillon's reunion with Roslyn. "So, what happens now?" Ava asked. "Do you all live happily ever after?"

"That's my goal," Dillon said. "Though I don't know what that looks like." He wanted Roslyn to move to Jasper, to move in with him, even, and the two of them to raise their child together as husband and wife. But he realized that was a lot of change at once, and might be too much for her to handle.

At the station the three of them walked in to applause. "Congratulations on stopping Kent Anderson before he injured more people," Chief Walters said.

"Thank you, sir," Dillon said.

"How is Ms. Kern?" Walters asked.

"She's been taken to the hospital for surgery to remove a bullet from her shoulder," Dillon said. "But the paramedic said she and her baby are doing well." He shot Brady a look. While word would spread soon enough that he was the father of Roslyn's child, he wasn't ready to repeat the story to the whole station. Not until he had at least told his family.

"The US Marshals Service isn't going to be happy you made them look bad," Captain Rutledge said. "They've been hunting for Anderson in Nevada."

"That's not on us," Walters said. "Come into my office, Dillon, and give me your verbal report. Then you can go home and get some rest. I imagine you need it."

Dillon followed the chief to his office and gave a recap of the past day and a half, including that he and Roslyn had had a previous relationship and he was the father of her child. "I would say that's a remarkable coincidence," Walters said. "But I've been in law enforcement long enough to wonder if there really is such a thing as blind chance. It sounds like you did a good job of keeping you both safe."

"Bentley deserves the most credit," Dillon said.

He looked down at the dog, who lay stretched out on the floor beside him, snoring softly. "He attacked Anderson when he fired at Roslyn and threw off his aim, and also distracted him long enough that I was able to overpower him. I'm also grateful Ava and Brady showed up when they did. I would have had my hands full trying to get both Roslyn and Anderson to the trailhead."

A knock on the door interrupted them. "Come in," Walters called.

Captain Rutledge stepped in. "The press is asking for a statement," he said. "I think Dillon should speak to them."

"It's your call," the chief said to Dillon.

"You'd only have to make a brief statement, maybe answer a few questions," Rutledge said.

He thought of Roslyn, dealing with the press on her own for so long. Maybe he could say something that would help her. "I can do it," he said.

From the chief's office he returned to the squad room, intending to start work on his report, but he was greeted again by both applause and hoots of laughter. "It's local heartthrob Dillon Diaz!" Jason sang out.

"The man on the US Marshals' Most Wanted list," Ava said.

"Our own Hunk of the Month," Cal said.

"What are you people talking about?" Dillon asked.

"According to the press you're a cross between a Chippendales dancer and a superhero," Brady said.

More hoots of laughter. Brady rested his hand on Dillon's shoulder. "Seriously, we're glad you're okay."

"We weren't really worried," Cal said. "I mean, who messes with the knight in shining armor who's rescued the damsel in distress?"

Dillon tried to smile, but all he could think of was that in a few minutes he was going to have to go out and face the people who'd written such preposterous things about him. He sympathized with Roslyn more and more. No wonder she hadn't wanted to reveal her real name when they first met.

Teresa hurried into the room. "There's someone here to see you, Dillon."

Before he could ask who, his mom and dad burst into the room. Or rather, Colleen burst—his dad followed at a more sedate pace. "Dillon, are you all right?" Colleen enveloped him in a perfumed hug.

"I'm fine, Mom. Really." He patted her back.

She pulled away, dabbing at tears. "I was so worried, especially when I heard you had to fight that awful man." She stepped back and looked him up and down. "Are you sure you're okay?"

"I'm fine, Mom," he repeated.

He turned to his dad, Ramon, who pulled him close in a tight hug. "It's good to see you, *mijo*," he said.

"And Bentley!" His mom had spotted the dog beneath Dillon's desk and knelt to pet him. "I'm sure you were a big help to my boy."

"Bentley saved us all," Dillon said. "He attacked Anderson and threw off his aim."

"So we know who the real superhero is," Brady said.

"I am going to cook you a nice big steak," Colleen said as she scratched Bentley's ears.

Dillon's stomach growled, reminding him how long it had been since he ate a decent meal. "What about me?" he asked.

"You can have a steak, too," Colleen said, and stood and took his hand. "Now, tell me about this woman. Roslyn."

"She's going to be okay," he said. "She's in surgery now to remove a bullet from her shoulder."

"She was shot?" Colleen placed a hand over her heart. "And you're not at the hospital with her?"

"I'm going there in a little while," he said. "When she's had time to come out of surgery."

Colleen studied him closely, then nodded. "You're in love with her, aren't you?" She held up a hand. "You don't even have to answer. I can see it in your eyes. You look exactly the way your father did when he and I were dating." She turned to her husband. "The way he still looks."

Ramon grinned. "Fast work, son," he said.

Dillon struggled to find the words to explain, aware that most of his coworkers were listening in while pretending not to. "Turns out Roslyn and I have known each other for a while."

"You knew her and you never said anything to me?" Colleen asked.

"It's a long story, Mom. We had lost touch."

"February!" Colleen tapped his arm. "That weekend you spent at the ski resort. I knew there was something different when you came back. You mentioned you had met someone, and then we didn't hear anything else. Am I right—Roslyn was that woman?"

He stared, unable to speak. His father gripped his shoulder. "I know," he said softly. "She scares me sometimes, too."

"The newspapers said she's pregnant," Colleen said. "Is that true? Who is the baby's father?"

"It's true," Dillon said. "And I'm the father." Saying it out loud in front of so many people made him feel a little light-headed.

His dad clapped him on the back. "Congratulations, again," he said.

His mother enveloped him in another hug, then kissed both cheeks. "You have made me a very happy woman." She dabbed at damp eyes again. "So happy."

Ramon put his arm around Colleen. "We'll go now," he said. "But we'll see you again. And call if you need anything."

Captain Rutledge came in as the Diazes were leaving. "The media are waiting in the conference room," he said.

He took Dillon's arm and hustled him into the conference room upstairs from the squad room.

The chief was already there, along with more than a dozen men and women with notebooks and cameras and microphones. Chief Walters, in full uniform, stepped up to the microphone. "Thank you all for coming this afternoon," he said. "I wanted to announce that Kent Anderson is in custody. Roslyn Kern is at Cascade Medical Center, where she is expected to a make a full recovery from a gunshot wound to the shoulder, a wound inflicted by Anderson before Sergeant Dillon Diaz of the Jasper Police Department, aided by his search and rescue canine, Bentley, subdued and arrested Anderson. And now I'd like to introduce you to Sergeant Diaz."

Dillon moved to the podium and gripped the sides, hoping no one would notice how nervous he suddenly was. "Hello," he said.

"Can you describe what happened out there today, Sergeant Diaz?" A woman in the front row of reporters asked.

Dillon looked toward the chief, who nodded. He took a deep breath. "Search and Rescue received a call about a missing hiker and my search dog, Bentley, and I responded." But really, the story had begun five months ago, when he decided to go skiing on Valentine's Day.

He summed up the events of the past two days as briefly as possible, then brought Bentley in to pose for pictures. The dog was happy to pose both with and without Dillon as long as Dillon kept feeding him treats. And Dillon was relieved to have some of the focus taken off himself.

"That's all the questions we have time for this evening," Chief Walters finally said. "Sergeant Diaz has been through a lot and deserves a rest."

He ushered Dillon and Bentley out of the room. "You should go home now," Walters said. "And I'm taking you off the schedule tomorrow."

"Thank you, sir," Dillon said. "I will go home, but then I plan to go to the hospital." He needed to see Roslyn. He needed it more than he needed a shower or a meal, though he would take care of both those things at home, if only so he could spend more time with her.

Chapter Seventeen

Roslyn awoke with a feeling of panic in her chest. She must have cried out, because someone laid gentle hands on her and a woman's soft voice said, "It's all right. You're safe and well."

"The baby?" Roslyn tried to feel for her belly, but medical equipment attached to her hands shortened her reach.

"The baby is fine," the woman said.

Roslyn's vision was clearing now, and she could make out a hospital room painted a soft blue. She turned to stare at the woman—a beautiful older woman with long red hair and bright hazel green eyes. "I'm Colleen Diaz," the woman said. "I'm Dillon's mom. I've spoken with the doctors and you're going to be just fine. The surgery went well. You'll be sore for a while but you should recover completely. In about four and half months you'll have no trouble holding your baby."

"They told you all that?"

"I told them you were the mother of my future grandchild." Colleen sat back. "They balked a bit at first, but I persuaded them to see it my way." She took Roslyn's hand in hers. "Since your own mother isn't here, I thought you wouldn't mind if I stepped in. No one should be in the hospital without an advocate."

Roslyn had to blink back tears. "Thank you," she said.

"Dillon will be here soon," Colleen said. "He was still busy at the station, but I know he wants to see you."

"You have a wonderful son," Roslyn said.

"I have three wonderful sons, but yes, Dillon is very special. And you must be special too, if you've captured his heart."

Had she captured his heart?

"I can see in his eyes how much he loves you," Colleen said. "You might think I'm imagining things, but a mother knows these things. One day you'll know them, too."

The door to the room opened and Roslyn's heart climbed into her throat as she looked toward it, expecting Dillon. But it was only a nurse, who checked her vitals and showed her how to operate the bed. The nurse nodded to Colleen. "I can see you're in good hands," she told Roslyn. "But if you need anything, press the call button and someone will come."

As the nurse was leaving someone else appeared in the doorway. Someone tall and broad-shouldered, whose face shone with a light when he looked at her. Roslyn's heart stuttered when she saw that light. Colleen was right—she knew. Did he see the same light in her eyes?

Dillon moved to the bed and kissed her forehead. "How are you feeling?" he asked.

"Groggy. A little sore." She tried to move her bandaged shoulder and winced.

"She's doing great." Colleen stood on the other side of the bed. "The doctor says she and the baby are in excellent health."

"Thanks, Mom, but I can take over now," Dillon said.

"You see how it is," Colleen said to Roslyn. "He wants to be alone with you." She waved goodbye and swept from the room. That really was the only way to describe it. Colleen Diaz obviously had a flare for the dramatic.

"I see you've met my mother," Dillon said.

"She's very nice."

"I'm not sure 'nice' is the word most people use to describe Mom, but she is a good person, if a little forceful at times."

"I think she and I will get along fine." *Because they both loved him.*

He leaned down to kiss her again, on the lips this time. "It's good to see you again," he said. "You frightened me for a little bit."

He had frightened her, too, when he launched himself at Kent Anderson. "Where is Anderson?"

"In jail, where he will stay for a long time," Dillon said.

"And Bentley! He saved my life."

"They don't allow dogs in the hospital. Not even heroes like him. He's home having a good nap." He settled onto the edge of the bed and gently held her hand, positioning around the IV.

He had obviously showered, shaved and changed clothes. "You smell good," she said.

"You look good. Not as pale." He traced her cheek with the back of his free hand and she fought the urge to lean into his touch, like a cat being petted. "I know you're tired," he said. "I won't stay too long."

She wet her dry lips. "I've been thinking."

"What about?"

"Maybe I could move to Jasper. I mean, I already know I like the town, and I'd like to be closer to you." She hurried to get the words out before she lost her nerve.

He didn't answer for so long that she was afraid she had misread everything. She felt panic rising. "I've got a better idea," he finally said.

"What's that? You don't want to move to Chicago, do you?"

"You remember I have a house. With three bedrooms and a big yard."

"Perfect for a family."

"We could make that family—you and me and our baby."

She swallowed hard. "It's a big step. Are we ready?"

"I think so." He moved their clasped hands to cover his heart. "I love you. I knew I loved you after our first day together. I don't want to lose you again."

She nodded. It was a big leap. But one she was ready to take. "I love you, too. And I want us to be together. So yes. Let's make that family. You and me and the baby. And Bentley."

He laughed. "And Bentley." And he kissed her again, their hands clasped now on the mound of the baby, a promise for the future. For forever.

* * * * *

K-9s on Patrol continues next month with
Scent Detection *by Leslie Marshman.*

And in case you missed the previous titles in the series:

Decoy Training *by Caridad Piñeiro*
Sniffing Out Danger *by Elizabeth Heiter*
Foothills Field Search *by Maggie Wells*

Available now wherever Harlequin Intrigue books are sold!

WE HOPE YOU ENJOYED
THIS BOOK FROM

HARLEQUIN

INTRIGUE

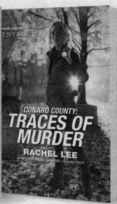

Seek thrills. Solve crimes. Justice served.

Dive into action-packed stories that will keep you
on the edge of your seat. Solve the crime
and deliver justice at all costs.

6 NEW BOOKS AVAILABLE EVERY MONTH!

HIHALO2021

COMING NEXT MONTH FROM

(H) HARLEQUIN

INTRIGUE

#2085 MAVERICK JUSTICE
The Law in Lubbock County • by Delores Fossen
Fleeing the hospital—and a deadly threat—Delaney Archer runs to Cash Mercer, the one man she trusts. Except the Clay Ridge sheriff and rancher hasn't seen the public defender in a year, not since Delaney ended their engagement. Can the Texas lawman shield her from a desperate killer... and the explosive truth?

#2086 SCENT DETECTION
K-9s on Patrol • by Leslie Marshman
Veterinarian Marie Beaumont's spent five years in witness protection hiding from a ruthless foe—until she and her K-9 save a handsome stranger with amnesia, who begins to remember her as the woman she once was. But is Jack a caring, electrifying protector...or a killer sent to finish off Marie, once and for all?

#2087 MISSION HONEYMOON
A Ree and Quint Novel • by Barb Han
Rule-breaking ATF agent Quint Casey is *this* close to nailing the ruthless weapons kingpin who murdered his first partner. But he and his undercover wife, Agent Ree Sheppard, are running a gauntlet of unexpected traps—and their wild-card irresistible passion for each other is putting everything at risk...

#2088 LAKESIDE MYSTERY
The Lost Girls • by Carol Ericson
LAPD detective Denver Holt doesn't know what to make of true crime blogger Ashlynn Hughes—but she has inside information that can help him crack his biggest homicide case yet. As anonymous tips carry them further into danger, Denver wonders if he can keep a target off Ashlynn's back...or if she'll be silenced for good.

#2089 SHIELDING HER SON
West Investigations • by K.D. Richards
Erika Powell has lived in hiding for years to protect her son from his wealthy, tyrannical grandfather. But when attempts are made on Erika's life, neighbor James West fears he may have endangered her—because the undercover PI's investigation of Erika might have led someone dangerous right to her.

#2090 REVENGE ON THE RANCH
Kings of Coyote Creek • by Carla Cassidy
The attack that lands Luke King in the hospital won't stop the Kansas rancher from bringing his father's murderer to justice. But when Carrie Carlson, the nurse who offers to join forces with him, narrowly misses being shot, can Luke fulfill his dangerous quest and keep her from the clutches of a vengeful killer?

YOU CAN FIND MORE INFORMATION ON UPCOMING HARLEQUIN TITLES, FREE EXCERPTS AND MORE AT HARLEQUIN.COM.

HICNM0622

SPECIAL EXCERPT FROM

⒣ HARLEQUIN
INTRIGUE

ATF agents Ree Sheppard and Quint Casey are
closing in on the criminal at the center of a weapons
smuggling ring they've been investigating while working
undercover. But once the bad guys are behind bars, will
Ree and Quint be able to transition their fake marriage
to the real-life relationship they're both craving?

Keep reading for a sneak peek at
Mission Honeymoon,
the final book in USA TODAY bestselling author
Barb Han's A Ree and Quint Novel series.

His hands cupped her face. She blinked up at him.

"They buried me," she said, fighting the emotion
trying to take over at the thought of never seeing him
again.

Anger flashed in his blue eyes, and his jaw muscles
clenched. "They better never touch you again. We can
make an excuse to get you out of here. Say one of your
family members is sick and you had to go."

"They'll see it as weakness," she reminded him. "It'll
hurt the case."

He thumbed a loose tendril of hair off her face.

"I don't care, Ree," he said with an overwhelming
intensity that became its own physical presence. "I can't
lose you."

Those words hit her with the force of a tsunami.

Neither of them could predict what would happen next. Neither could guarantee this case wouldn't go south. Neither could guarantee they would both walk away in one piece.

"Let's take ourselves off the case together," she said, knowing full well he wouldn't take her up on the offer but suggesting it anyway.

Quint didn't respond. When she pulled back and looked into his eyes, she understood why. A storm brewed behind those sapphire-blues, crystalizing them, sending fiery streaks to contrast against the whites. Those babies were the equivalent of a raging wildfire that would be impossible to put out or contain. People said eyes were the window to the soul. In Quint's case, they seemed the window to his heart.

He pressed his forehead against hers and took in an audible breath. When he exhaled, it was like he was releasing all his pent-up frustration and fear. In that moment, she understood the gravity of what he'd been going through while she'd been gone. Kidnapped. For all he knew, left for dead.

So she didn't speak, either. Instead, she leaned into their connection, a connection that tethered them as an electrical current ran through her to him and back. For a split second, it was impossible to determine where he ended and she began.

Don't miss
Mission Honeymoon *by Barb Han,*
available August 2022 wherever
Harlequin Intrigue books and ebooks are sold.

Harlequin.com

Copyright © 2022 by Barb Han

HIEXP0622

Get 4 FREE REWARDS!

We'll send you 2 FREE Books plus 2 FREE Mystery Gifts.

FREE
Value Over
$20

Both the **Harlequin Intrigue®** and **Harlequin® Romantic Suspense** series feature compelling novels filled with heart-racing action-packed romance that will keep you on the edge of your seat.

YES! Please send me 2 FREE novels from the Harlequin Intrigue or Harlequin Romantic Suspense series and my 2 FREE gifts (gifts are worth about $10 retail). After receiving them, if I don't wish to receive any more books, I can return the shipping statement marked "cancel." If I don't cancel, I will receive 6 brand-new Harlequin Intrigue Larger-Print books every month and be billed just $5.99 each in the U.S. or $6.49 each in Canada, a savings of at least 14% off the cover price or 4 brand-new Harlequin Romantic Suspense books every month and be billed just $4.99 each in the U.S. or $5.74 each in Canada, a savings of at least 13% off the cover price. It's quite a bargain! Shipping and handling is just 50¢ per book in the U.S. and $1.25 per book in Canada.* I understand that accepting the 2 free books and gifts places me under no obligation to buy anything. I can always return a shipment and cancel at any time. The free books and gifts are mine to keep no matter what I decide.

Choose one: ☐ **Harlequin Intrigue**   ☐ **Harlequin Romantic Suspense**
                  Larger-Print   (240/340 HDN GNMZ)
                  (199/399 HDN GNXC)

Name (please print)

Address   Apt. #

City   State/Province   Zip/Postal Code

Email: Please check this box ☐ if you would like to receive newsletters and promotional emails from Harlequin Enterprises ULC and its affiliates. You can unsubscribe anytime.

Mail to the **Harlequin Reader Service:**
IN U.S.A.: P.O. Box 1341, Buffalo, NY 14240-8531
IN CANADA: P.O. Box 603, Fort Erie, Ontario L2A 5X3

Want to try 2 free books from another series! Call 1-800-873-8635 or visit www.ReaderService.com.

*Terms and prices subject to change without notice. Prices do not include sales taxes, which will be charged (if applicable) based on your state or country of residence. Canadian residents will be charged applicable taxes. Offer not valid in Quebec. This offer is limited to one order per household. Books received may not be as shown. Not valid for current subscribers to the Harlequin Intrigue or Harlequin Romantic Suspense series. All orders subject to approval. Credit or debit balances in a customer's account(s) may be offset by any other outstanding balance owed by or to the customer. Please allow 4 to 6 weeks for delivery. Offer available while quantities last.

Your Privacy—Your information is being collected by Harlequin Enterprises ULC, operating as Harlequin Reader Service. For a complete summary of the information we collect, how we use this information and to whom it is disclosed, please visit our privacy notice located at corporate.harlequin.com/privacy-notice. From time to time we may also exchange your personal information with reputable third parties. If you wish to opt out of this sharing of your personal information, please visit readerservice.com/consumerschoice or call 1-800-873-8635. **Notice to California Residents**—Under California law, you have specific rights to control and access your data. For more information on these rights and how to exercise them, visit corporate.harlequin.com/california-privacy.

HIHRS22

HARLEQUIN

Heartfelt or thrilling, passionate or uplifting—Harlequin is more than just happily-ever-after.

With twelve different series to choose from and new books available every month, you are sure to find stories that will move you, uplift you, inspire and delight you.

SIGN UP FOR THE HARLEQUIN NEWSLETTER

Be the first to hear about great new reads and exciting offers!

Harlequin.com/newsletters

HNEWS2021

Love Harlequin romance?

DISCOVER.

Be the first to find out about promotions, news and exclusive content!

[f] Facebook.com/HarlequinBooks

[Twitter] Twitter.com/HarlequinBooks

[Instagram] Instagram.com/HarlequinBooks

[Pinterest] Pinterest.com/HarlequinBooks

[YouTube] YouTube.com/HarlequinBooks

ReaderService.com

EXPLORE.

Sign up for the Harlequin e-newsletter and download a free book from any series at **TryHarlequin.com**

CONNECT.

Join our Harlequin community to share your thoughts and connect with other romance readers!
Facebook.com/groups/HarlequinConnection

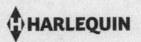

HSOCIAL2021

**IF YOU ENJOYED THIS BOOK
WE THINK YOU WILL ALSO LOVE**

**HARLEQUIN
ROMANTIC
SUSPENSE**

Danger. Passion. Drama.

These heart-racing page-turners will keep you guessing to the very end. Experience the thrill of unexpected plot twists and irresistible chemistry.

4 NEW BOOKS AVAILABLE EVERY MONTH!

HRSXSERIES2020